I0570857

Shivers

CIRO

REMMY DUCHENE

Ciro
ISBN # 978-1-78430-272-6
©Copyright Remmy Duchene 2014
Cover Art by Posh Gosh ©Copyright October 2014
Interior text design by Claire Siemaszkiewicz
Totally Bound Publishing

Published in 2014 by Totally Bound Publishing, Newland House, The Point, Weaver Road, Lincoln, LN6 3QN, United Kingdom.

Totally Bound Publishing is an imprint of Total-E-Ntwined Limited.

CIRO

Dedication

To Ericka Walden, Jade Baiser, Havan Fellows, Vanessa Womble and Big Papi— Thank you for your years of encouragement and Virtual hugs. And to Lil Miss and JW, I couldn't have written this without you.

Prologue

"From the deepest desires often comes the deadliest hate."
— *Socrates*

Ciro sat in the main hall of Olympus listening to the chatter around him. It was the last place he wanted to be, as he wasn't a god by any means. But, since Zeus was his father, he was forced to sit with Ares, his brother, to the left, and his sister Aphrodite on the right, with all the other gods of Olympus at a meeting that was dragging. Even Hades sat, glowing in dark robes, looking as though he was bored to death. Glancing around the room, Ciro noted no one seemed as interested in the gathering as Zeus was. Often, Ciro would turn to see Hera watching him intently. The goddess unnerved him and she probably wished he would just die. He was a constant reminder of her husband's many weaknesses.

But that was not all. One moment she disliked him, the next she was trying to seduce him. He knew what she was up to, and Ciro wasn't going to fall for it. Forget for a moment the disgust he would feel sleeping with his father's wife, but letting her seduce him would harm his mother. Ciro wasn't about to be entangled in the feud between Zeus and his wife any more than he had to. To be honest, he liked it better when she was trying to kill him. At least that way he knew how to fight back.

His mind switched gears to his brothers. A few of them were fine—they lived a life away from Earth and Olympus. Those brothers chose to remain silent, mere blips in the fabric of existence. Though Ciro couldn't do that, he refused to destroy the people his mother cared about. They were, after all, a strong people. Then there were the other brothers who had come out wrong. They were hellbent on world domination. Ciro had spent his adult life fighting them off, but he was tiring.

Finally, Zeus hit the giant lightning bolt he held against the side of his chair, signaling the end to all their torture and dragging Ciro back from the journey his mind had wandered on. He simply turned his head to watch the others push their chairs away. The motion caused the legs of the seats to scrape against the floor as everyone rose. They dispersed, but Ciro remained where he was, massaging his temples.

"Are you staying, brother?" Ares asked. "If not, I could use your assistance."

"I do not think I can feel my brain," Ciro replied crossly, tapping the sides of his head with his index fingers. It really did feel as if his brain had gone to sleep—or was frozen.

Adrestia laughed and kissed Ciro's cheek. "You are so theatrical, Uncle Ciro. But I must go—there is a war looming and I must stop it. Now, do behave while I am away."

Ciro smirked at her telling him to be good since he was so much older than she was. "You? Stop a war?" he questioned then turned to his brother. "Am I missing something, Ares?"

"It boggles my brain too," Ares replied.

"It is not a beneficial war, dear uncle. There is no balance or revenge needed in this case. The crime was not committed." Adrestia flipped her hair dramatically. "I hate to see innocents suffer because their leaders are morons. I must show my face and forbid it. Yes, Father, I shall take Osaki with me. But if he requires a recharge…"

"I understand." Ares made a face but smiled.

Before exiting the room ahead of Hercules, Adrestia hugged her father then kissed Ciro's cheek again. Ciro shook his head.

"What is bothering you?" Ares fell back into his seat. "You seemed a little more preoccupied than usual. Sisqo told me one of the rogues got a jump on you the other night. Do not make that a regular occurrence, brother."

"Trust me, Ares. I do not intend to make it a regular thing. My head just was not into the whole patrolling thing and he came out of nowhere."

"Okay. So what is on your mind?"

"I am not certain," Ciro replied softly. "It is as if each time I take one step forward, I am pushed four leaps back. It is a rather trying sensation."

"You are not making much sense, Ciro."

"And that is how jumbled it is inside my head." Ciro inhaled and held the breath before exhaling long and hard, causing the door to shake. "I fear I am losing my touch, Ares. I have been hunting Gala for the past six Earth months and he has managed to elude me at every turn. I mean, what am I doing wrong?"

"Listen to me. Just because you have yet to catch him does not mean you are losing anything. Some nuts are just harder to crack than others—as the humans always say. What are your options when it comes to fighting him?"

Ciro shrugged. "I am out of options. It seems I have tried all there is to try."

"No." Ares shook his head. "I do not accept that. There has to be something we are missing."

"With Kost, it was not this hard. He was very easy to track and once I found him…"

"Yes—but…"

"Yes, yes, the nuts being harder to crack—I get it. I fear my brothers are growing stronger and soon I will be unable to stop their destruction."

"That does not sound like you," Ares said, leaning forward to speak so only Ciro could hear. "You cannot give up. Gala has been a challenge. I will not dispute that. He stepped into being in the midst of a war I was waging against the Badlands and drowned all my soldiers."

"I am sorry about that."

"Stop apologizing for their actions. You know, the other gods ask me how I can be such friends with humans and the answer is simple. They have idiosyncrasies that work well in this situation. They say every adult human is responsible for his or her own actions."

"But they are not humans."

"I know but it applies. They are adults—not children. Every decision we make has consequences, Ciro. Your brothers are not above that and they will have to learn this lesson or die. After they drowned my soldiers, Hades was not prepared for such a deluge of the dead and he, too, was upset with me at first. Plus a part of Terra was left under the sea so both Gaia and Poseidon were unhappy with that concept. Who rules that part of Terra that was not originally underneath the ocean?"

Ciro rubbed his eyes. Suddenly they were throbbing—a rather unusual sensation. He rested back on the seat and stretched his legs out before him.

Ares continued, "Our brother is causing too much damage. So far, the other gods have remained out of this battle, because you have asked them not to interfere. But you have to strike now, Ciro."

"I know." Ciro dragged his fingers through his hair. "I know they will not remain patient for much longer. I have been asking too much of them."

"I understand you believe this to be your responsibility, Ciro. But there is no shame in asking for help. Needing someone to stand by your side is not an act of cowardice, for it takes a brave and wise being to know when he requires someone's aid."

Ciro understood that but didn't believe it applied to him. Still, he nodded.

"If you wish some assistance from myself and Adrestia," Ares said. "You know we are more than happy to help."

"This is my fight. Gala is my brother…"

"Yes, and he is also mine—but you have not heard anything I just said about asking for help, have you?"

"I have." Ciro's voice cracked, so he cleared his throat. "But this is truly my fight. My powers match his. I must do something before he lays ruin to Earth or even here—but especially Earth. Mother would be heartbroken."

"I understand. In the meantime, I must ask your help with something."

Ciro turned to eye his older brother. "Sure, anything. You know that."

"I shall be going into battle with Cerepides." Ares shifted in his seat.

"Say no more. I shall bear arms with you."

Ares nodded, and the two men rose. They headed toward the door as Zeus shouted Ciro's name.

The brothers exchanged looks.

Ares patted Ciro's shoulder. "Do you wish for me to stay? I know how much you…"

"Do not worry, brother. I can do this."

"I shall await your arrival."

"I shan't be long." But Ciro wasn't so sure. Each encounter with his father generally left him in a foul mood that went on to alter any plans he had beforehand.

Ares didn't look convinced. Ciro offered him a smile, and Ares nodded, dragged his fingers through his long hair then strode from the room.

Finally, Ciro was alone in the main hall with the creator god. Ciro had never liked him. Though Zeus had sired him, he'd also hurt Ciro's mother irreparably, and that was something Ciro could never forgive.

"I wanted to have a word with you about Gala and the rest of your cursed brothers," Zeus said. "The damage they can cause on Earth is insurmountable."

"You never cared for the humans before, Father," Ciro snapped. "Why the sudden concern for their safety?"

"Insolence! What is that supposed to mean?"

"It means whatever you wish it to mean." Ciro was tired and bored with the interaction. Zeus' little talks never made him feel anything but anger.

"The humans are in danger and we both know it."

"They are just people to be tricked into sleeping with you and nothing else, right, Father?" Ciro questioned. "This little back and forth is getting us nowhere. Why do you wish to speak about my brothers?"

"Do not be impertinent."

"Father, impertinence is a human emotion. Something you find alluring—was that not what you told Hera?"

Zeus seemed to be at his wit's end. He dragged a hand over his face and down his dark beard. He picked up the long folds of his robe and shoved them away from his feet as he stormed toward his throne. Ciro stood rigid, watching his father until Zeus sat and faced him.

"You have no reason to be like this with me."

"Do I not?" Ciro asked, stepping forward, fists clenched. "You caused me to be what I am. You, who could not be faithful to the goddess that he chose as his wife, caused this—all of it. You do what you like whenever you like—and to Tartarus with the consequences. You have no regard for human life, and yet they worship you. How does it feel, oh mighty Zeus, to betray the same people who look up to you for guidance?"

"That is *not* what any of this is about."

Thunder crashed around them as Zeus' voice echoed through the grand room.

"Yet, once again, you refuse to take responsibility for your raging cock. Father, do you not see what is happening? I have to kill my brothers. Do you not care how that makes me feel?"

"Why should I? You are not one of my claimed sons."

Ciro hung his head slightly with a smile on his lips and shook his head. "And once more, you've managed to sink lower than even Hades himself. The honest truth, *Father,* is that Gala's destruction is on *your* head."

"Don't you dare speak to me like that. I am your father."

"Then act like it," Ciro yelled.

A strong wind blew through the room from his ire. Zeus' hair danced with the force of the air, and he even staggered backward in obvious shock.

"Your brother has been a menace."

"My brother? He is *your* son. *You* caused this. You go places you should not. You sire offspring then you leave them there for whatever poison Hera's sick little mind can think of. Remember Hercules?"

"If it wasn't for me, you would not be alive, so I would appreciate some gratitude."

"Yes, dear Father," Ciro spat. "I forgot. You and I have a very different understanding of what *alive* means. You stay away from Gala."

"He is terrorizing people on small islands, sending downpours and heavy winds, and you cannot seem to find him or stop him."

"I am working on it."

Lightning sizzled through the room before charging off the columns stretching upward to Zeus' chair. The white streaks ran along the floor toward the door then disappeared. Zeus' anger must have been at its tipping point to cause that. Though others would cower in a corner, Ciro lifted his head and met his father's fiery eyes with defiance.

"I do not care how you do it," Zeus spoke between clenched teeth. "Either stop this *thing,* or I will."

Though he didn't particularly like his brother Gala for all the damage and pain he'd been causing, Ciro knew he had to be stopped. Yet, he still didn't like

Zeus threatening Gala or calling him a *thing*. They were brothers, after all. His hatred for the creator god intensified, but he knew there was very little he could do about that.

"I am only going to say this once more. Stay away from my brother. He is *my* problem."

"Or what?" Zeus demanded.

Ciro's eyes flashed lightning. The small bolts crackled inside his head then flicker off his eyelashes. "Or you will see the true strength of Hera's curse."

Zeus eyed him for a moment, eyes emotionless, face expressionless. "If you cannot fix the issue, or put a leash on your brother, I will."

Ciro frowned. He never had responded well to ultimatums, especially when they came from Zeus. Instead, he turned on his heel and stormed out of the large slabs used for doors. He hurried down the airy corridors with the rounded windows overlooking the heavens on one side and Aphrodite's palatial gardens on the other. He peered out to see if he could catch a glimpse of his sister, but had no such luck. She was probably off somewhere with Ares or just wandering around with Athena.

Using his mind, he called for Ares.

"I am on Earth, brother. War waits for no Shiver."

"My apologies." Ciro chuckled. *"I shall come to you this instant."*

"Why must you provoke your father so?" Hera's voice swam over him, leaving a disgusting shiver down Ciro's spine.

"You know how he gets." She was always lurking around like some kind of snake. Why *wouldn't* she be eavesdropping on his argument with her husband?

Normally, he didn't fall for her bait but he stopped and turned to look at his stepmother. "Provoke him?

That is rich. Today seems to be a very backward day. He wants to go after Gala, and you are standing up for him—when did this happen?"

Hera laughed softly, a sickening sound that always made him feel as if he was being touched by evil. "No matter what he does, he is my husband."

"And since you are so understanding, why am I like this? On second thought, do not answer that. I must go."

"Ares is always in trouble or some sort of war. He is more than capable of handling himself. He *is* the God of War, for crying out loud. Stay a while. Talk. Eat."

Ciro gave his stepmother a look he wished would kill her and stormed toward the east wing of the main structure. When he was close to the wall, he glanced over his shoulder at Hera then disappeared.

Chapter One

Ciro sat before his mother in the Hall of Winds and tilted his head. She grinned at him and patted her hair gently.

"Do you like it?" she questioned. "I thought I should change it up a bit after so many years."

He smiled. "It is very becoming, Mother," he replied, reaching over to touch her hand gently. "I truly like it."

"And yet you seem unhappy."

"I am." He couldn't hide anything from her. Though her wrath could be devastating to anyone who tested her, Thýella was a loving mother. Perhaps she was too kind, for now most of her children ran amok among the very people she cherished so dearly. "There is something unpleasant I wish to speak with you about."

"I think I know what it is."

"In the coming days, I will have to hunt more of my brothers," Ciro began, swallowing a lump rising in his throat. "They have posed unnecessary risk to Terra. Gaia is not pleased and has tasked me in setting my brothers straight. But you and I both know they would rather die than be kind to humans. What should I do?"

"You know what must be done, Ciro. You are the eldest."

"Mother—they will not stop with just a mere defeat. It has been proven repeatedly in the past. They keep right on coming."

"Then they must die..." Thýella lifted her head, elongating her neck, a stern look filling her eyes. "They are my children, and though I love them fiercely, they have disappointed me so desperately. I cannot deal with Gaia's wrath. And she would be right in being angry and seeking retribution for their damage."

"Ciro!" The second eldest ran into the room. "We have trouble."

"Who is it?"

"Gala."

Ciro's heart broke. He gritted his teeth and stood. "I was hoping to reason with him but the more I think about it, the more I know that will never work."

"You cannot reason with a mad man," Koi said sternly. "You were the one who taught me that, brother."

Ciro nodded, gave himself a moment to pull himself together then offered his mother a sorrowful look. "I must go, Mother."

"I will come with you," Koi told him. "Two is always better than being alone."

"No," Ciro said. "Stay here with Mother. If he gets past me, he may show up here. I need someone I trust to protect her."

"I assure you I can protect myself." Thýella raised her chin.

Koi continued as if Thýella hadn't spoken. "You trust me?" he asked in a soft voice.

He touched Koi's cheek then patted it. "We will talk later. Please stay here."

Koi did not look impressed, and after pressing his lips into a thin line, he nodded stiffly.

Accepting a kiss to his cheek from his mother, Ciro took a moment to breathe. With a final look at Thýella, he exited the luxurious room and began his descent to Earth.

Once he landed, Ciro knew something was about to happen. There wasn't much time to look around and take stock of anything, or even call for assistance. Usually, he had a little leeway to get Ares, Adrestia and Hygeia to help him clear cities and towns. In this instance, he had no such luxury.

Ciro bent his knees, digging his feet into the ground just before pushing upward. He flew through the air with his arms by his sides and his chest mere inches away from the tall structure before him. He climbed higher, up the side of the tallest building in the city bordered by two small towns. Darkness swarmed above, as though Hades had risen and tossed a blanket over everything.

He felt it then—the charge of lightning flashing from his eyes caused by the stench of evil carried on the wind. The breeze howled, surging from the north, and Ciro knew it was going to be bad if he didn't figure out what to do—and fast. With his coat flopping behind him in the breeze, Ciro stood atop the one-hundred-and-eighty-story building. He tried figuring out where the attack would come from. Tracking had not been easy. When he was led to one of the small towns in the east, it almost broke his heart. The town was quiet, lovely, perfect.

Children ran along the streets calling to one another. A little boy kicked a ball so hard it flew over a fence, hitting an old man on the side of the head. The man only laughed and handed the ball back.

A couple of dogs chased each other down a back road, barking happily at their game. Lovers lay on towels and blankets on what the locals called the beach, which was merely a lake with a sandy shore.

On the far side, workers had used heavy equipment to pile large rocks into the water so people could sit on them to watch the sunset. Ciro knew if something was to happen there, the place would be devastated. The citizens would lose everything and the town would be wiped off the map. In order to stop it, the only idea he could see was to lead his prey away from the perfection he now watched to somewhere larger, to somewhere he would have more room to navigate and stop the attack.

Something pulled Ciro from his thoughts, snapping his head upward. Though it was dark, a scent filled the air that he instantly recognized — danger. Suddenly, it was there before him. He saw it the moment the funnel shape started forming. Pressing his thumb and forefinger of his right hand together, he then dragged his thumb down his index finger. A white streak of lightning followed his thumb while he frowned. He shoved his left hand out, sending a ball of lightning from his palm that disappeared within the funnel. A growl of pain followed, but it didn't stop the turmoil.

Ciro made a face then looked down. Below him, he discerned the panic. People were running, trying desperately to get out of the way. But the funnel cloud simply grew bigger. The larger it got, the more fear Ciro detected from the crowd beneath him, making him slightly ill. He tried shocking it a second time, which only slowed it before it sped up again.

That was precisely what his foe wanted—to see the humans running around, scattering like headless chickens in their fright. Gala fed from their misery, which made no sense since he was not a god of pain. He wasn't even a god, but a tributary of one. Ciro was instantly sick and disappointed. His brothers were powerful beings but they were weak from their cruelty. Gala didn't care how harming the humans made his mother feel. Ciro knew that for certain.

"I see Mother sent her favorite son," Gala spat. "Predictable—as always."

"That is not how it is and you know it."

"And how do I know that, Ciro? Whenever something goes wrong, she sends you—as if you are god and creator of us all."

"That is because you act like a child. You do things—these things…" Ciro motioned around him furiously. "Then you expect her to welcome you with open arms."

"She does not welcome me at all," Gala snapped.

"I am not in the mood for these games, Gala," Ciro thundered, his voice echoing through the heavens. "Your pity party is not one I wish to attend."

Gala's anger sent a jolt of lightning downward. When it hit the ground, the earth shook slightly and a gaping hole appeared at the landing sight.

"That is enough," Ciro yelled. "Stop this madness now!"

"But I am having so much fun," Gala teased. "Why should I give that up?" A face pushed out from the side of the twister and smirked at Ciro. "Because you love the humans? Why do you think it so important to protect them? When are you going to learn we are better than they are? When are you going to accept that they are merely insects in our paths? Crush them like the insignificant beings they are."

"That decision is not your call. They are Mother's prized people and what you do breaks her heart. Do you not care?"

"Mother is weak. Is that not why we are here? Her weakness to fight Zeus? Come now, brother, surely you see that as clearly as I do."

Ciro growled. "She is your mother. What you do puts us all in jeopardy with Gaia. Now either stop this madness, or — "

"Or what?"

"Be destroyed."

"You wouldn't. Mother will not allow it."

"Oh, Gala, so young and so naïve. Mother has made her choice. She chooses her people. But with or without her blessings, I know you have to die."

"You do not scare me, Ciro. Your bark is worse than your bite. Besides, you love family too much to harm me."

Why do they always tempt me so?

Ciro lowered his head slightly but kept his gaze on the funnel before him. Gala's face had disappeared into his creation again. Brother or not, Gala was a threat and Ciro would be damned if he allowed this joker to destroy another town or city because of his god complex.

Raking his hair from his face, he looked down one last time at the people scurrying back and forth. Pieces of concrete were breaking off structures and hitting the ground. Ciro watched as a chunk struck someone and they fell, to lie still.

"Hygeia — I seek your assistance," he called to the Goddess of Health.

She instantly appeared, beautiful and glowing in white. He smiled sadly at her before pointing downward. Hygeia nodded.

"I shall try and limit your work," Ciro promised. "In the meantime, please help them."

"I will, my friend. Go and do what you have to do."

With those words, Ciro jumped from his perch. He disappeared then reappeared in the center of the funnel. True to form, Gala emerged out of thin air and instantly attacked. Vanishing, Ciro came into view again behind Gala, sending a kick to his back. Gala fell forward and vanished. Inhaling, Ciro turned in time to slam a foot into Gala's chest right as he reappeared. Gala flew across the space and fell out of his funnel. Soon he was back. His powers hadn't developed as strongly as Ciro's, so he couldn't shimmer out of view as fast as Ciro.

"I warned you," Ciro said between gritted teeth. "Now you pay the price."

The fight was fierce like a strange yet beautifully choreographed dance. The power of their exchanged blows caused the twister to grow stronger, and lightning charged across the space a little too close to the ground. Ciro knew if he didn't end the battle soon, his worse fears would come to pass — another town would be swallowed by the spinning inferno and there would be nothing Hygeia could do to help. Defeating Gala seemed impossible. He countered each of Ciro's blows, following them with attempts of his own, but Ciro was becoming impatient.

A wise friend's voice swam through his mind. *"When it comes to fighting, my friend, patience is a virtue."*

Ciro took a fist to the chest and staggered backward. Gala didn't seem to want to give him time to recover, for he attacked again. Turning away, Ciro grabbed

Gala's arm, spun him around and slammed his palm into Gala's back. He pushed forward slightly, sending a bolt of lightning through Gala, who stiffened in Ciro's arms, jolted, then slumped in the air. Ciro hovered over him, watching him twitch before he finally faded from view. A low hum filled the air and he recognized it as Gala's soul leaving his body. It sparkled with blue light but only for an instant before turning black and slipping through the earth.

Ciro took no pleasure in his enemy's demise. He knew each time he destroyed a Shiver, there were still more out there, ready to take his place. Gala was right. This battle he was waging to protect the humans was becoming more and more futile with each opponent. Rising higher than the funnel, he opened his palms toward it, forcing it to heed him. Bowing his head, he watched as Gala's creation dissipated and calm was restored. The dark gave way to light and people began making their way outside once more. Homes weren't badly damaged, but a few things had toppled over. Most of the carnage was relegated to the higher buildings.

Hygeia had changed herself into a human woman and was assisting people on the ground. Ciro couldn't land and lend a hand, for humans were easily spooked and unpredictable. He took a breath and shook his head, hungering for peace and rest. Even as he vanished, Ciro knew the rest he craved would never come to him.

Chapter Two

After the freak storm the day before, Carter Olabasu was sure they wouldn't be able to use the basketball court the next morning. But when he woke, it was dry enough to play on. He was happy for that, because he needed the time with his brother. He went up for a jump shot, but the basketball merely spun around the rim of the basket and fell to the ground. Kofi picked the ball up and tossed it to Carter. The two went back to their in-depth conversation about love and forever.

"You know you're a dick, right?" Carter asked, dribbling the ball in place with his free hand on his hip.

Kofi grinned and yanked the ball away before shooting a three-point shot to the basket. "Yeah, but a dick you love."

Carter thought of so many dirty comebacks that he could counter with, but decided not to rock the boat. Kofi was still getting used to the idea that his younger brother was gay. Smiling instead, Carter caught the ball and walked back to the center of the court.

"You love the idea of being *in* love. I know that about you." Carter dribbled it a few times then stopped. "But you're telling me if you find someone you really love that you wouldn't give up everything for her? Even if you knew there was no one else out there like her—I mean sure, you'd be able to find someone who comes close, but not quite—know what I mean?"

Kofi looked thoughtful for a moment before walking to the side of the court and grabbing his towel. Carter watched his brother with an arched eyebrow, wondering what was going through his head.

"Okay, check this out right here. There are two things that are for sure in all of this," Kofi began slowly. "One, you are never certain about love. It's all trial and error—often times its just error and you have to let it crash and burn. What do I mean by that?" Kofi pre-empted the question before Carter had a chance to ask. "Let me explain—you could meet someone and you two love each other, confusing it with being *in love* with each other, then a few years down the road— *voila*, splitsville."

Ciro tilted his head. "And two?"

"Two what?"

"You said there were two things you're sure of in all of this. You gave me one, what's the second thing?"

"Oh," Kofi said with a small smile. "Yeah, and two… We're never certain about people. We have this pesky little thing called free will and sometimes we use it to take advantage of a situation. The only thing we can be sure of when it comes to human beings is that they will, at some point, hurt or disappoint you. How many times do you hear a woman claim the child is her husband's then something goes wrong, like the child needs a life-saving operation or blood transfusion—and wham! Not the father. Giving up your whole life for someone could then come back and bite you on the you-know-what."

"Yeah but now you're being overly dramatic."

Kofi lifted the bottle toward his lips and stopped. "Am I?" he asked, then drained the bottle and hurled it into a nearby recycle bin. "Just think about it."

"I *am* thinking about it. Not everything is that black or white. Sometimes there are gray areas in the middle—areas that can make a situation better if you only look for it."

"That's just it—if it was meant to be, you shouldn't have to look for the gray. It's either there or it's not."

"Okay, fine—people disappoint you. But you can't keep living your life where you're so paranoid that you don't meet and experience people."

"Carter, it's not like that. I'm not *that* jaded."

"Right." Carter nodded sadly. "I know I let you down in the worst way. Don't deny it. I see it every time you look at me. Like this morning when I opened the front door. You had this expression on your face like *damn – not again.*"

"Carter…"

"No. Let's be honest here. When we were kids, we agreed there wouldn't be any lies between us."

"We were children."

"But still," Carter interrupted. "We had a point. As I was saying, when I told you I was gay, I saw your world burned to the ground. Dramatic? Perhaps. Still, it doesn't make it any less true. But are you going to sit in a corner with your face to the wall, hands over your ears, ignoring the urges in your body because you're terrified a woman may drop another man's child in your lap?"

"Maybe not. But the thought will be in the back of my head."

With a roll of his shoulders, Carter ventured over and grabbed his towel and water. He drank half the contents of the bottle before screwing the lid back on then placed it on the bench. Passing the towel over his face, he thought carefully about Kofi's words. Though he could still find faults in his brother's argument, Carter sat beside his bottle and watched Kofi, who was busy staring across the way to the mountain.

"It's been almost a year. I know you don't want to talk about this," Carter broke the silence between them. "Eventually we will need to face things, then you'll have to make a decision on whether you want me around or not."

"Don't say that." Kofi turned. "Of course I want you around. You're my brother. I need you in my life."

"It's not that simple, Kofi. I can't keep seeing your sadness whenever you look at me."

"I know. I know." Kofi sighed and sat beside him. He stared through the mesh fence at the houses below.

"We don't have to right now. I just wanted to let you know that sooner or later we should, you know?"

"I just… It's still a shock to me that you're gay. You were always the one who got all the girls—and you're gay? I don't understand it. It's proof to me gay isn't something you choose." Kofi faced him. "They were sexy women."

Carter smiled. "I know you're disappointed and that was the last thing I ever wanted to do…you know, make you look at me as something of a failure. It damned near killed me when it did happen. It was like I was punched in the chest, and for a bit there, I couldn't breathe right."

"Nah. It wasn't disappointment. I'm sorry you saw that. I was just stunned—one of those getting-hit-in-the-back-of-the-head-with-a-two-by-four kind of surprises."

Carter snorted and shook his head. It wasn't the first time he'd heard someone say that about him since about being gay.

"You love who you love, Carter." Kofi's voice was softer now, serene. "And since you're my brother, I have to love who you love. So far, you've kept your men away from me, and I really appreciate that."

"There hasn't been any—I haven't dated since I told you." Carter bowed his head. "I didn't want to push the issue or make you feel like I was shoving it in your face or anything. It was bad enough with my confession. I can do without men, but I can't live without you. Look, I haven't really been with anyone anyways. I just didn't want to get in too deep, because I know how unsure you are of the whole thing."

"You put your heart aside for me?"

"Kofi, with all due respect, don't ask that," Carter whispered. "You're my brother. That means something—hell, that means everything to me. I already put too much on you. I didn't want to bring someone home, then have you come over, see him and know precisely what we were doing. I couldn't take the chance I'd lose you any more than I already had."

There was nothing else to say. That one simple sentence was all that was needed. Silence echoed across the court, making Carter's head hurt a little. The faint sounds of trucks wafted up the hill from the center of the valley and, from somewhere off in the distance, a dog barked. A gust of wind blew around them then disappeared down the other side of the hill.

"You never lost me, Carter. I've always been right here. Sure, I fought the idea of you liking men rather than women but I never really paid attention to how much my standoffish behavior would affect you. I'm sorry." Kofi took a breath and shifted against the bench. "I'm ready now."

"Kof…"

"Listen to me," Kofi said. "The same way you never wanted to be a disappointment, I never wanted to do that to you, either. You're my baby brother. I should have your best interest at heart. For a moment, I lost sight of that. This isn't how our parents raised us. We know better."

Carter inhaled sharply.

"Gay or not," Kofi continued before Carter could speak, "I'm here for you. I've got your back. I am so ashamed of what I've put you through. I can't ever ask you to put your happiness—your heart—aside for me."

"You didn't ask." Carter shook his head.

"Not in words. But we're being honest with each other right now, aren't we?"

Carter nodded while rubbing his palms against his thighs.

"The way I acted didn't give you much of a choice," Kofi whispered. "Damn, I was so selfish. How in the hell did I ever think this was about me?"

A short silence spread between them. The quiet was interrupted only by the faint, periodic sounds of vehicles moving down at the foot of the hill. Kofi inhaled sharply, a noise that carried its way to Carter, who turned to look at his brother.

"I never want this to happen again—this miscommunication between us." Kofi's voice broke. "Especially when it comes to your happiness. I don't want you to misunderstand how I truly feel. I made you believe it would hurt me to see you with someone and for that, I'm really sorry. I shouldn't have acted the way I did, and Lord knows, I feel like shit for it. Date. See what's...I mean, who, is out there. Seeing you happy means a lot to me."

"You sure?"

"Yes. It took a while, but I'm ready."

"All right. The next one."

Kofi laughed and patted Carter's back.

"What about you?" Carter asked.

"What about me what?"

"Kofi, I haven't seen you with a woman for a while now. I want you to be happy too, you know?"

Kofi nodded. "I know. I just— Lately I haven't been interested. I guess I haven't seen a woman who pulls me in. I don't know how else to explain it. But whatever *it* is, I really wish it would go screw itself."

Carter laughed.

"I have to go if I'm going to get any work done in the office today. All I want to do right now is take a nap, though."

Carter stood. "You can sleep when you're dead— isn't that what they say?"

"Well, obviously the jackass who came up with that deserved to be shot," Kofi said, hugging his brother.

"I think he's already dead, bro."

Kofi pushed his lips upward in a slight pout then shrugged. "I'll call you later about dinner and what we're doing tonight."

Carter agreed, then watched as his older brother exited the gates of the private basketball court then disappeared into the house. He should to go after him, maybe give him a couple of bottles of the wine Carter had received from a wealthy client a few days prior, but he decided to remain where he was and take in the fresh morning air. He ran a hand over his head and drew a deep breath. For that moment, all he wanted to do was just sit there and think about nothing, to clear his mind and enjoy a momentary lapse in existence.

As usual, what he wanted didn't matter to his heart, for the crushing weight of his loneliness swarmed him. He opened his eyes quickly in panic as the feeling threatened to consume him. It was as if he'd been tossed into a pool, not knowing how to swim and he was slowly sinking. Carter gasped. He had money and a brother who loved him dearly, but it wasn't enough. Sometimes, the loneliness got so overwhelming Carter began to believe he was becoming a hermit in his house on the hill.

Carter had remained celibate. He just hadn't been able—in all good conscience—to go and find a man knowing how badly it would hurt Kofi. The sex wouldn't feel right and everything else would just be as though he was on the down low again. He didn't like hiding his sexuality in the first place, so forcing himself back into the closet wouldn't be good for anyone.

Now that he had Kofi's blessing, he desperately wanted to see what was out there—maybe even find someone to share his life with. After all, there had to be something more to the life he was currently living. His cell phone vibrated from where it lay on a pair of socks, but he didn't move or even look at it. After repeated rounds of trying, the person or persons on the other end must have figured out he wasn't about to answer and gave up. He didn't bother checking to see who it was. If it was important, they could leave a message and he would check it later.

Finally, he pulled himself from inside his head and looked down at his watch. His eyes bulged. It was an hour later and he was still sitting on the court where his brother had left him. With a frown, he walked back to the house. He took some time to shower and dress, then was out of the door again in no time.

The ride to work was boring, the silence threatening to drive him mad. Even as he made his way into his office and flopped into his seat, he didn't feel any better. Still, Carter forced himself to work, forced himself to finish the sketches that needed to be done. Being in and out of meetings didn't help either, but he felt a little better knowing the meetings were successful, with two multi-million dollar projects coming his company's way.

By the time Kofi called at close to four in the afternoon, his spirits had lifted a little. "Listen," Kofi said "there's a party tonight at Firewall. You in?"

"You want to take your gay brother to a club full of women?" Carter grinned impishly.

"I would tell you to kiss the blackest part of my ass, but I know you're joking. You in or what?"

Carter thought about it. He was never a partier on the best of days. There was something about crowded rooms and bad music blasting from speakers with everyone gyrating against each other that just didn't sit well with him. It always left him feeling like a sardine in an already overstuffed can. Still, it was a better offer than what he had planned for the rest of his night. He was going to head back to the house, watch some boring reality show reruns while working some more over a beer then go to bed. That was all there was to do in his life at nights. He felt like a failure and it was the worse feeling he'd ever experienced.

"I'm in. What time?"

"Atta boy. Pick me up at about eleven. I'll get us VIP."

"Aight," Carter jargoned. "And Kofi?"

"Yeah, bro?"

"Please be wearing pants when I get there. We both know your ass is always late."

"I promise nothing." Kofi laughed. "Besides, no club really gets hopping until after midnight anyway. That's when all the hunnies come out to play." He hung up.

'I promise nothing' was Kofi code for *'don't hold your breath.'*

Carter finished his day and hopped back into his car for home. He suddenly didn't feel much like a party, but he had promised Kofi. He felt like they were as they used to be—close, almost sharing a brain, which used to drive their mother crazy. He smiled at the memories as he turned his car left down Hollington for the highway.

Their mother Prentice Olabasu had been a beautiful woman. Carter remembered the deep brown of her eyes and the slight pout of her lips. Her hair had always been immaculate and she'd smelled of either jasmine or juniper. He was too young to know why she'd always looked so put together but as he'd gotten older, he understood. She was keeping herself up for their father. Even that hadn't been enough to keep the man around. The moment he'd found out she was pregnant again, he'd taken off. Carter hadn't known his father and his mother didn't like talking about him. When Carter had been a bit older, she'd sat him and Kofi down and had explained it to them. Carter used to find himself apologizing for what their father had done, but Kofi had always rolled his eyes and walked away. It was a heavy load to carry—the load that his mother was alone because of him. For years, Carter had felt as if he'd shattered his mother's very soul. Though she never once blamed him, Carter never felt any less culpable.

It was only later that Kofi told Carter it wasn't his fault.

Carter stopped at a local mall and entered his favorite little bookstore.

"Carter Olabasu." The blond woman, who looked akin to a hippie, ran around the counter to hug him tightly. "I'm glad you stopped by."

"Why is that, Jeanne?" he asked, returning her hug.

"We're going out of business."

"Why? Business is good, isn't it?"

"Yes, especially since we started selling those ebook things. But the rent in this mall is killing us."

"Well, instead of shutting down, have you thought of moving the store out on its own? You have regular customers who will come to you as long as the place you move to isn't in the middle of nowhere. Just across the street there's a standalone building for lease. I know these things. My brother is a real estate agent, remember?"

Her face lit up. "You know? I didn't think of that and neither did our damn lawyers. But it's a good idea. Shutting down this business broke my heart and I don't know what I would have done with myself."

Carter grinned. "Look into it. It would be a shame, because no one around here knows where to find my rare books."

Jeanne laughed and patted his back. "You're a good man, Carter O."

"I try. Find out about the conditions of the lease and let me know. I'll come back and give the place a onceover for you, if you'd like. No charge. Or better yet, my brother is the brains behind the sales, so why don't I ask him to help you out?"

"You would do that?"

"Of course. I told you. I love coming here. You always make me feel so welcome and I don't want this little store to disappear."

Tears welled in the woman's eyes, and Carter gave her a hug he hoped would comfort her.

"I'm so happy right now." She cried into his shoulder. "Thank you so much. You made my day."

With their conversation over, he found the books he wanted on Spanish architecture, had her order a few more for him and, after paying, he continued on his way. He used his hands-free to call Kofi about what he'd told Jeanne and it didn't take long for Kofi to agree. The truth was that Carter knew his brother hated seeing small businesses go under as much as he did, because of things like financials. It was a no-brainer to help Jeanne.

At home, he checked his messages, fielded a few calls from some very paranoid clients and made some dinner. He had a craving for pasta, so he filled a pot with water and placed it on the stove to boil. Afterward, he set to work chopping up the ingredients he needed from onions and green peppers to garlic and thyme. Soon the kitchen smelled like a spice shop. By the time he was finished cooking, he didn't feel much like eating. Carter served himself a small amount, poured a drink and forced himself to eat, since he'd skipped lunch. He took a little time to clean up then sat to watch some television.

Chapter Three

Sitting on the Boat of Charon would cause a human to weep and moan. It was the Barge of the Dead, the one to carry their souls to Tartarus and into the presence of Hades. Yet he sat on it, eyeing his brother as the vessel swayed ever so slightly in the water. "How many souls came to you today that weren't supposed to?"

"Eight," Hades replied softly. "One of our brothers caused a tsunami off the southern coast of Japan. It is not storm season there — they were not prepared."

"Damnation."

"Ciro, we have to do something."

"We are — I just cannot seem to sense them as quickly as I used to and I am not quite certain why that is."

Hades eased back in his chair and it squeaked in protest. Ciro could go into Tartarus to visit but it was a painful experience, one he tried desperately not to do too often.

"Perhaps you should seek a break," Hades suggested. "Let us handle your brothers while you are away."

"It would not be any kind of a break, Hades. I would be constantly worried about what they were up to. I would come back even more stressed than I am right now."

Hades shook his head, his dark locks swaying from side to side. "You have been running ragged for so many years. I could keep an eye on things for you."

"I appreciate you offering, still, I cannot. There is so much to do. But if I need your help in a fight..."

"What is it the children are saying these days? I got your back?"

Ciro chuckled. It was true—he'd heard that before and a few other variations. It was strange to hear Hades, God of the Dead, say it.

"I know what the humans think of me. They think me greedy and mean, that I would take a soul just to grow the number of my subjects. But the fates do not like it when peoples' destinies are rewritten and killing humans before their clock runs out is doing just that. We do not have much more time before the fates get involved, and when they do, it will be completely out of our hands."

"You would think after Gala, the others would stop because of that one fact alone."

"What I don't understand is why they are like this," Hades mused. "You have the same curse they do—and Koi and the others. So why all this destruction?"

Ciro shook his head. "I have been wondering the same thing. Mother says it is because I am eldest, but I am not sure if that is true anymore. Aerios is as strong as I am."

"I am not certain what to say to that, brother." Hades rose and walked to the edge of the boat. He stared down into the darkness of the Acheron river and inhaled. "But whatever you do, you best do it fast. The waters are restless."

"What does that mean?" Ciro stood beside him. He stared into the water but he couldn't see anything except black, murky liquid.

"It means something bad is about to happen and I really hope it has nothing to do with one of our brothers."

Ciro pressed his lips into a thin line.

"I wish I could simply take their life forces and end it now. But that is not how it works. I may be the keeper of the dead but even I have no power over death. No one visits me here. Often times it's lonely."

"You have all these souls here…"

"Yes. I'm never alone, but I am often lonely. There is a difference, brother." Hades stopped speaking for a moment.

Ciro said nothing.

Hades continued, "There is a fear of what I am, what I do and what this is. Even the Gods of Olympus fear it all. I cannot blame them. But sometimes I would like to see their faces here."

"It's the finality of death, Hades. There is just something about it that makes everyone run scared."

After giving his brother a hug, Ciro left him there on the Barge of the Dead and made his way back to land. He didn't stick around long on Earth. His next stop was Olympus.

"Hello, beautiful sister," Ciro greeted Aphrodite.

The goddess was busy staring intently into her love pool while twirling her fingers within its waters. She turned around and a smile lit her face.

"Oh, brother, you are such a sweet-talker." Aphrodite rose to kiss both his cheeks. "But I adore you for it. I am terribly sorry for Gala."

"And what do you have to be sorry about, dearest?"

"That he put you in the situation where you had to take his life. Brothers should not be warring with each other. Use Zeus as your example."

"But we are of our father's blood, Aphrodite. Why should we be any different? And if we chose not to follow in his footsteps, why then should we be happy?"

Aphrodite smiled softly and nodded. "You are troubled, dear brother, which makes what I have to say more dreadful."

Adrestia and Hygeia entered the room.

Adrestia made a face. "Why must you be so dramatic, Aphrodite? It cannot be all that bad."

"Dramatic? I do not think it dramatic. Besides, I think a little over embellishment now and then is good for the heart."

"What is this horrible news, Aphrodite?" Ciro pushed.

"Our dear brother is about to fall in love," she said, her voice filled with sorrow. "How absolutely heartbreaking."

"Heartbreaking? That's wonderful news," Ciro replied. "I thought your job is to celebrate love? Why would that be a bad thing?"

"It is my job to celebrate love," she responded. "But not when it's bad news for those I love."

"Besides," Hygeia spoke up, walking to look into the pool, though no one else could see what was happening but the Goddess of Love. "We gods and goddess are known to fall in love constantly—

sometimes with people or beings we have no right falling for."

"That's just it." Aphrodite looked into her pool again. "I keep checking and rechecking and the end result is always the same. I really do not see a way around it."

"Aphrodite...please..." Ciro pleaded. "Just tell me why you believe my falling in love is such a bad thing. The wait is killing me."

"Yes," Hygeia added. "Do not leave us in suspense. We are all dying to know what this dreadful news is."

"Ciro is about to fall for a human," Aphrodite all but cried.

Ciro laughed. "That will not happen, dear Aphrodite. Perhaps your son Eros has gotten into your lines again and is playing a practical joke. I was told by the Oracle of Olympus my love is not mortal but a demigod."

"My son has not been in Olympus in over a fortnight."

"Then there has to be another explanation," Ciro told her. "The oracle is never wrong, so your pool probably needs cleansing."

"She is this time—wrong, I mean."

"But Aphrodite..."

His sister snapped her head up and she leveled a glare on him. "Are you saying I am incorrect, Ciro? I know what I saw."

"That is *not* what I am saying. I think you may be mistaken. Perhaps it is Koi who is meant to fall in love with a human—or Aerios."

She said nothing else and stormed from the room. Ciro exhaled loudly and looked to Adrestia and Hygeia for help. Both goddesses shrugged and he knew they had nothing to say that would make the situation better. He shook his head and exited the room, desperate to find Aphrodite. She was easily offended and sometimes he forgot that fact. Regardless, it didn't make sense for him to have a human for his lifemate.

Ciro continued searching for her but after he couldn't find her, he gave up and went back to his chambers to grab a few things. It was time for his rounds anyway and it wouldn't be fair to ask Hercules or one of the others to take his place. He would have to speak with Aphrodite later.

"Ciro, before you go," Hygeia's voice stopped him from leaving.

He turned to see her standing at his door, leaning on the frame.

"Your essence is weak, my friend," Hygeia continued. "Perhaps you need some rest."

"There is no time for that, Hygeia."

"You cannot keep this up forever. One day you will have to stop—one day you will have to rest. It is not for the weak and there is no shame is asking for assistance."

"I will remember that. Thank you."

Hygeia smiled. "Your fight with Gala."

"Yes?"

"He is dead."

"Yes. I received confirmation from Hades soon after. It broke me having to do that, but I had no choice. I am responsible somehow for them and the evil they do."

"But you are but one Shiver, Ciro. Though you are powerful, you cannot do it all or stop them all. They are your brothers, not your children."

"And yet they behave oh so much like children."

Hygeia approached slowly, her long gown brushing the floor. She touched his cheek gently. "I see the sorrows in your eyes, Ciro. I know your pain, for I can feel it beating through my very heart. It devastates me to see you so unhappy. I wish nothing but the best for you and your brothers. You did not ask to be a part of Father's twisted little lies."

"But here I am. Father takes no responsibility in the hurt he causes—never has—and I hold out no hope he ever will. Even with Hercules and Perseus, he created the chaos and flies off like a pixie filled with vigor for the next mischief while we all suffer the consequences."

Hygeia allowed her hand to fall away from his face. "Do not let your father's crimes visit you, Ciro. I will not allow that to happen. You are a good sort. If you need someone—anytime—you just call."

Ciro smiled sadly and nodded. "I must go, dear friend."

"Ciro..."

But he just couldn't stay or say anything else. So many unshed tears welled up behind his eyes. If she showed him any more kindness, he wasn't sure he would be able to control them. For hundreds of years he'd held them back, refusing to show weakness. But that all seemed to be slowly building, swelling like a dam within him, threatening to burst.

His descent to Earth was a slow one, for he stopped in the Hall of Winds to check on his mother. She was busy playing a game he'd never seen or heard of before with one of her friends from the Wind Aisle. Koi was off somewhere or other with Hercules. Ciro kissed her cheek, bowing his head to his mother's friend in farewell and continued on his way.

The night was slow and after his patrol, Ciro went off shift, leaving his best friend, Sisqo, to do his rounds. There was something in the air — something that seemed to be taunting him. It came and went with the wind like a small spray of cologne or a puff of bad-smelling smoke. Though he couldn't quite put his finger on it, he called in to the others and pulled himself off-duty so he could be with Sisqo. Since Sisqo was still working, Ciro spent the time in deep conversation with Hades and reported to Earth after Sisqo's rounds were over.

He sat in the semidarkness of the VIP section and watched the dancers on the crowded floor. The need to be close to strangers never appealed to him. Perhaps it was because he hadn't been intimate with someone in a long time. Why he chose to go to a straight club was beyond him. Well, at first he'd thought it was a great idea because he figured he wouldn't get his ass grabbed, pinched or slapped. But those things happened the moment he walked in the door.

"I'm telling you, it's crazy out there," Sisqo said, closing the VIP door behind him. "All those bodies — the air is electric. You really should get out there."

"Not my scene, really."

"You are no fun — you know that?"

Ciro laughed. "I am here, am I not?"

"Yeah, yeah." Sisqo grinned. "How was your patrol?"

Ciro thought of the question and shrugged. "Same old. Nothing went bump in the night, but I keep smelling trouble, feeling it on the air and not seeing anything. Even now as I sit there, I can taste it. Either my powers are being blocked by something or I am just losing my mind."

"Losing your mind? Damn it."

"What?"

"You already went crazy. Is it possible to go crazier?"

"You, my friend, are a dick."

"I've been told. Anyway, I didn't feel anything. So unless I'm getting old or losing it too, then there's nothing to worry about."

"Maybe." Ciro rubbed his sore ass. "There is just something wrong with this picture."

"You didn't think this one through, did you?" Sisqo asked with a smirk.

"Not quite. I figured at a straight club I wouldn't get my ass pinched so much—I was wrong."

"Well, don't worry. A good-looking man is a good-looking man, so you can't fault them for grabbing your ass. The women obviously saw something they liked."

Ciro laughed. "And you think I'm good-looking, Sisqo?"

"Yeah, I don't swing the Shiver way." Sisqo grinned.

"Yes, you do."

Sisqo laughed aloud. "True but I like my men, less—less, Shiver-y."

"You're an ass."

But Sisqo the demigod formed his fingers into the shape of a heart over his chest then pointed at Ciro. Shaking his head, Ciro finished his drink then propped his black boots on the center table beside his empty glass. Work swam into his mind, even though he was trying to breathe and let the worries of the world leave him, at least for a little bit. Each time he closed his eyes and tried to forget, he realized how miserably he was failing at not thinking of work. He glanced at his coat draped over the back of one of the plush seats, debating within his head if he should just leave and do another round. It would be better than just sitting around listening to music he'd never understand in a million years and feeling irritable.

He was about to rest his head back when he caught a strong, alluring and delicious scent. His mouth watered, causing him to swallow convulsively. He rose slowly and walked to the velvet rope. There had to be some mistake. Aphrodite couldn't be right, for that would mean the Olympus Oracle was wrong — the oracle was never wrong.

So many naughty thoughts flew through his mind as he stared out of the glass — each one of them hotter, sexier than the last and every single one turned him on. His body throbbed in ways he'd never felt before with any of his other lovers. His cock pressed against the front of his pants, leaving him trembling. Even with this reaction, Ciro still couldn't figure out where the smell was coming from. He ached to know more about the being who possessed the intoxicating, almost hypnotizing, bouquet. On the other hand, it scared him. Something had to have gone wrong with the oracle's predictions. There was no other way to explain what he was feeling for this human.

Every Shiver had a reading because their species was so new and different. Most times, it was just a regular thing, like a two-dollar psychic playing about with tarot cards. But Ciro's reading had been different. Pain and hardships filled his, but the one part of his that caught him the most was that he was to fall in love with a demigod — the fates had spoken it. All his life he'd thought the demigod was Sisqo, but he didn't have any sexual attraction to his friend. Then he would spend nights lying awake just wondering if he would ever find this mysterious demigod the oracle spoke of. Lover after lover, close call after close call—Ciro had finally given up.

He sat motionless and let his gaze wash over the crowd until he found the source of his new obsession. This man didn't have the smell of arousal toward the sexily clad women around him like a good ninety percent of the other men. It could mean either he was gay or Ciro was just missing something. Ciro watched him cross to the bar and take a stool. The black dress pants the man wore were just tight enough to show off muscular thighs. The stranger looked lovely in a matching baby-blue shirt that flowed over chocolate skin.

With a smile, he allowed his body to shimmer from the room and appear behind the stranger. Everyone was so obsessed with grinding against one another that they hadn't even noticed what he'd done. The music blared around him. Patrons walked back and forth, a few bumping into him. Soon, he couldn't hear the music and his body was knocked from the left then the right by gyrating forms. Everything became a dull hum and all he could really feel was the way his body pulsed at the mere smell of this man. It had to mean something—he had to take a chance. A part of him knew this human could never be his one true mate—how could he be? Humans were unpredictable and panicked. Before he could stop himself, he tapped the sexy morsel on the shoulder.

"Can I buy you a drink?" Ciro asked him.

The man tilted his head and peered up at him. Confusion filled his brown eyes. For a moment, Ciro thought he was wrong, but when the dark-skinned beauty licked his lips, Ciro knew the man before him was aroused.

"Is that a regular question you ask a man in a straight club?" The guy wanted to know, mischief dancing in his brown eyes.

Ciro smiled. "Well, if you are straight then I will apologize and buy you a drink anyway."

"Smooth-talker…"

"So I have been told."

"Okay. You can buy me a drink," the stranger said. "Black Velvet."

"I am Ciro Pyktis."

The man leaned in, bracing a palm on Ciro's chest and spoke in his ear. "Carter Olabasu. Nice to meet you."

Ciro did not want to break that connection between them. With the simple action of a hand on his body, a spark of electricity surged through him. It traveled up his chest, grazing his neck before he realized he must come off as a bit creepy to Carter. Ciro reluctantly stepped away. He hoped Carter believed it was to order their drinks, but Ciro knew better. He knew the spark would crackle through his eyes and he wouldn't be able to control it. It would freak the human out, and the last thing Ciro wanted was to be away from him. For Carter's drink, Ciro watched the bartender dump some ice into a glass, followed by some champagne then some Guinness.

So that's what a Black Velvet is.

Returning to his catch, Ciro noticed a vacant stool but he figured he'd like to get Carter in a private area where he could speak to him without yelling. He accepted their drinks and handed Carter a cold glass. Before he had a chance to say anything else, he realized another man was trying to get Carter's attention.

"I was going to ask you to dance but I think he's trying to speak with you."

"He? Who?" Carter looked genuinely perplexed and turned to look.

Ciro bowed his head and smiled sadly. He was always attracted to the wrong men. Perhaps it was because Aphrodite had told him the man of his dreams was indeed a full-blooded man and not half. Maybe that was why he thought he smelled his lifemate. Carter obviously had someone else. It was probably for the best. With the war happening between himself and his brothers, a human wasn't a good thing to have around. It still sucked not being able to feel Carter against him, around him and inside him. No matter how he thought of it, his heart broke at the thought of having to walk away from this man without so much as a taste of him. What he wouldn't give to watch Carter's big brown eyes change with fire and dazed with pleasure. Again, he had to force his mind from where it was going. The more he thought of Carter, naked and panting under his body, the more Ciro felt a piece of him slowly withering away.

Taking a breath, he glanced around and stepped back, allowing the crowd to swallow him.

Chapter Four

Carter saw his brother then whirled around to speak with Ciro, the spot beside him now occupied by someone else. Ciro was nowhere to be seen. Frowning, he eased from his seat with his drink in hand and walked to where Kofi stood waiting for him.

"You have the worst timing, you know that?"

"What? It's not like you found booty. It's a straight club."

"How would you know? You just swept right in, and he probably thought you were my man or something." He didn't want his irritation to show. A part of him thought Kofi had interrupted on purpose, but he quickly took a deep breath and pushed that thought out of his head. Kofi would never cock block him on purpose. Carter's body was beginning to rebel. He thought for sure if he pulled his pants down, his balls would in fact be blue.

"I'm sorry. This is a straight club, remember? How should I have known?"

"He was hot though — and he bought me a drink and was going to ask me to dance until he saw you. Couldn't you have waited a few more minutes?"

"Yo, sorry, bro. Like I said, I didn't think you would pick someone up here. I'll go somewhere else while you find him and talk to him, okay?"

"It doesn't matter now."

"Well, obviously it *does* matter, because you have this look in your eyes. I know it's been a while..."

"Kofi..." Carter shook his head.

"I'm sorry."

Carter sighed. Perhaps it was the fact he hadn't been laid in so long he was sure his body was overheating on him. The good-looking man who had bought him a drink had done something wonderful to his whole being, and that irritated Carter. It all boiled down to one thing — it wasn't really Kofi's fault. Then again, he was so damned rusty when it came to men and their ways that he probably would have fucked it up before he could blink. Still, he looked back to where he had been standing with Ciro and couldn't help feeling a bit of loss at the thought Ciro was so beautiful and interested. He shook his head and shrugged.

"It's all right." Carter sighed and shook his head. "It wasn't like we were going to get married or anything. What's up?"

"Just wanted to see if you wanted to get outta here," Kofi said. He didn't look convinced with Carter's surrender.

"You wanna leave? I didn't even see you dance with that many girls." Carter glanced around, hoping to see Ciro again but the lighting in the club wasn't conducive for a search mission. In fact, the flashing lights were beginning to give him a migraine.

"Not feeling it tonight," Kofi replied. "Seriously, you want to leave? If you want to stay, I can catch a cab home."

"No. No… Might as well go home."

For most of the ride home, neither man spoke. After a while, it seemed Kofi couldn't take the silence anymore. "I really am sorry, you know? I wasn't trying to break up your flirtation or anything. Damn, am I that out of practice that I can't tell when two people are flirting?"

"I said it's all right, Kofi. Just let it go. You're putting too much thought into this."

"Then why are you still so sullen?"

"I'm not sullen," Carter replied. He checked the mirrors before switching lanes. "I'm just sad. For the first time in almost three years, a man was interested in me and I could actually show some interest back, then I look away for a second and he's gone. I just feel as though I don't have *it* anymore, you know?"

"Wait, you think you're not desirable? Is that what this is about?"

"Like I said, it's not that big of a deal. I don't even know if it makes sense in my own damn head. Forget about it."

"No. I'm not going to forget about it. How can you think you're not desirable?"

Carter said nothing. He really didn't feel that comfortable yet having these kinds of conversations with his brother. A part of him still knew a little bit of Kofi wasn't copacetic with the whole homosexual deal, so he bit his lip and turned left onto Kofi's street.

"Dude, this is a really awkward conversation to have with my brother."

"Carter."

"Leave it alone, Kofi. Please."

"Fine…but we're picking this up later."

Carter didn't doubt they would. Kofi was always the one to push the issue when it came to conflicts between them—though rare. He was not looking forward to part two of that conversation. They stopped in front of Kofi's house but Carter didn't feel like going inside. He just wanted to go home. He just wanted to be alone.

Shifting the car in park, he relaxed in the seat, hands by his sides and stared over at his brother who looked straight ahead.

"Can I ask you something?" Kofi questioned.

"Sure."

Kofi nodded, turning his attention to Carter. The look on his face told Carter something was wrong.

"How—how did you know you were gay?"

Carter tilted his head. "Kofi…"

"It's just a question."

Carter licked his lips and thought about the question for a bit. Then he just shrugged. "I don't know. I supposed I always knew. When I looked at women, I appreciated their shape and the softness of their skin. I thought they were—are—beautiful. But when I looked at a man I saw sexy and yearned to be touched… It's not easy to explain."

"Oh."

"Why?"

"Nothing," Kofi replied and pushed from the car.

"Kofi." Carter stepped from the vehicle and rested his hand on the roof. "Now *this* is a conversation we'll be picking up later."

Kofi merely lifted a hand in the air but didn't stop to answer. He hunched his back like a man carrying the weight of the world on his shoulders. Carter wasn't sure why. He knew Kofi wasn't gay—there was no way he could be. When Carter came out, Kofi didn't take it well. Maybe it was because Kofi had always been into women, beautiful, educated, legs-for-days kind of women so he expected Carter to be as well. Whatever the reason, Carter knew Kofi wasn't at all pleased.

After his brother had closed the front door, Carter fell into the front seat again and headed to his place. The moment he was through the door, he stripped off his dress shirt. He placed it over the back of a chair — something that would cause his mother to cringe if she ever saw it — then undid his belt. He pulled it from the loops of his pants, hurled it to the chair and trailed a hand over his now tightening nipples. Each time he thought of the stranger, his body reacted in ways he'd never felt before.

"This is nuts," he muttered.

They'd only spoke for a minute. Still, Carter could remember how hard the man's chest was under his hand. The moment he'd touched Ciro, his pecs had twitched beautifully against Carter's hand. He couldn't believe the way he'd reached in, pressing into this man he hadn't known more than a few seconds. But there was something so right about it, especially when he'd felt Ciro's heart race against his fingers.

Ciro had smelled of sandalwood and leather and just the memory of those aromas sent images of being bound and helpless beneath Ciro's mouth, tongue and fingers flying through his mind. The scary part was those images did not make him flinch or feel ashamed. Instead, they sent his body into overdrive. His nipples tightened further with every brush of the air against them. He pulled them between his thumbs and forefinger, squeezing then pinching. Releasing them, he took a breath and flicked the tight, tender buds with his nails.

"Oh, damn." He sighed.

A groan left his lips when the wind passed over his aroused flesh, leaving him weak in the knees. Somehow, Carter's brain told his feet to move and they obeyed, carrying him up the stairs to his bedroom where he switched on the radio. Love songs floating from the speakers caused him to frown deeply. He wanted something to take his mind off the bulge in his pants and the hammering of his heart. But no such luck, because Kofi had touched his damned presets again. Sighing, he allowed Shawn Desman to continue singing the song *Shiver*.

Meanwhile, everything about Ciro filled his thoughts, from his black hair and mysterious silver-gray eyes, to his large shoulders, which Carter wanted to brace his legs on while taking Ciro deep within his body. Everything about Ciro gave off an aura of raw sexuality. It was hard to find a man like that, and Carter couldn't believe his crummy luck. He stared down at his bed. Suddenly he wasn't tired and didn't want to crawl between those sheets alone again. It was either go to bed or drive himself crazy thinking about some stranger he'd never see again.

Lying back in his bed, he trailed a hand over his hard nipples, across his chest then down his abs. When he circled his cock with his fingers, he arched his back, moaning, and stroking ever so slightly. He licked his lips, squeezing harder, tugging and twisting his wrist. The curtains blew inward, sending a slight gust of wind into the room. He wanted to stop, to get dressed and ignore the burning sensation in his body, but he couldn't. The sensations flowing through him were too beautiful. He'd gone without the touch of a man, even his own caress, for too long.

He imagined Ciro over him, touching and tasting him. He was using his full lips to drive Carter mad, and Carter welcomed it. It was good to feel something carnal again, great to know he hadn't forgotten what it was like to allow his body access to pleasure. All Carter could do was release his cock and give over to the sweet feeling of delicious pleasure threatening to drown him.

The wind picked up slightly, howling like a song through his room, flowing over his skin like a lover, caressing him softly. It left a hint of goosebumps over his flesh, making him shiver slightly. There was nothing better than the remnants of a tremble flowing slowly down Carter's spine, through his veins, all the way down to the very tips of his toes.

"Oh, damn…"

Carter glanced at his dick. It was twitching and growing. He'd never experienced anything like it. His cock danced before his gaze, daring him to do something. Writhing, he slipped back down and the urge to yell tore through him. He bit against his fist, trying to stifle the feeling. Instead, it only grew stronger. The fire was so intense that without touching himself, his dick erupted, sending spurts of white liquid flying through the air. A number of shouts, foreign to his ears, ripped from his throat repeatedly. Carter's toes curled his eyes rolled back in his head and every part of his being trembled with the force of his beautiful undoing. The warmth of his climax reached his chest and abs. As his body burned sweetly from the drops of cum, Carter could hear Ciro's voice, low and husky, carried to him on the wind.

"That's a good boy…"

Carter lay staring at the ceiling, chest heaving. Having an orgasm while thinking of a man he'd only met for a few seconds was new to him. He didn't feel guilty about it — only confused. It made no sense. Why would he do that? Maybe he was thinking about Ciro too much — putting too much thought into it. The simple explanation was that he hadn't had sex in years and his body was finally telling him to go fuck himself.

Yes, that had to be it. There was no other possible reason for the way he'd just reacted and what he'd done.

He wanted to clean up, but his limbs were too weak to move. It would have to wait.

Chapter Five

Ciro burst into his house and pushed out of his jacket. His chest burned from breathing rapidly, and he crashed into a table. A blue vase older than time itself smashed onto the ground, but Ciro didn't care. His body was on fire and nothing he did would stop it. He pressed his back against the wall as someone tried holding onto him. He pushed them away and staggered into the kitchen. His body shimmered out of view a few times before slamming painfully into the counter. That kept him in the room, at least for the moment.

"Ciro," Sisqo hollered. "Are you all right? Were you attacked?"

"No—water…"

"Yeah, sure."

Moments later, a cool glass was shoved into Ciro's hand and he downed the contents before handing it back. "More."

After his third glass of water, Ciro braced his back to the counter and forced himself to stand in this time and space. His body kept shimmering in and out of existence.

"Ciro, focus. You can't keep phasing out like this. It's going to drain you," Sisqo called, smacking Ciro hard across the face. "Come on. Look at me—look...at...me."

He pressed his eyes closed and tried to regain control of his body. Soon, he was breathing somewhat regularly again. "I did something...all I had to do was walk away, but I could not. Now, I have crossed that line."

"What did you do?" Sisqo questioned. "I've never seen you like this before."

"He was just so damn sexy and I wanted him so desperately. I never felt anything like that before—such raw, pure need."

"You mated with a human? Cee, you've done that for years—decades. What's so different about this one? What did you do?"

Lifting his eyes to look at his friend, Ciro groaned and shook his head. The truth was that the moment he'd sensed Carter Olabasu, he should have run the other way. He should have downed his drink and left the ground that Carter was on, but he just hadn't been able to leave. His scent, the thought of his beautiful dark skin, those large, kissable lips and the wide, manly shoulders, left Ciro feeling like a teenager again. "I can't..."

"No, you're not going to start this conversation and then stop part way. What did you do?"

Ciro walked off with Sisqo calling after him, but he didn't stop until he made it to his bedroom. He locked the door behind him and flopped back on the bed. As he stared at the ceiling, the room spun slightly around him. Gripping the sheets, he closed his eyes and waited.

This too shall pass.

This has to pass.

Shit, what have I done?

Yet, he wondered about Carter. He couldn't seem to stop his mind from going there. What would he say if Ciro told him who he truly was? Would Carter run away or would he try to make things work between them? The sex would be tremendous. Ciro knew that for sure. Just one whiff of him and all Ciro wanted was to rip Carter's clothes off, bend Carter over that bar and drive into him hard from behind. That primal feeling was something Aphrodite had warned him about many years ago.

"Love? What is that?" Ciro had asked her.

She'd shrugged while brushing her long, dark hair. "It is something we all should feel at some point in our lives. It is beauty and happiness and light."

"When do you know you're in love?"

"When you feel wild with the person—almost primal. Then you'll know."

Ciro had shaken his head. "That makes no sense."

"It will," Aphrodite had said, kissing his cheek then skipping from the room.

Ciro frowned, wondering why that memory was so hard on him. He would love to be Carter's man, to feel the way his body throbbed and pulsed while they had sex. But it wasn't all about sex, it couldn't be. There had to be more to all of it.

As the night gave way to early morning, Ciro still hadn't gotten any sleep. His eyes burned terribly. All he wanted to do was roll over and go back to dreamland, but he couldn't even get that. The moment he closed his eyes again, something rippled inside his head and he frowned. His brother Ares was calling for him. There was an urgency in the summons that made Ciro groan. After pushing his frame off the bed, he grabbed his coat then climbed out of the window and disappeared.

When he reappeared, he was on Olympus. Ciro strode into the room, with his jacket blowing about his ankles, and looked around. The regulars were there but he sought one in particular. During his quest, he stopped to have a conversation with Hades. The two were surprisingly close, since Hades didn't particularly like anyone.

"Have you seen Ares?" Ciro asked.

"He is around here somewhere. I saw him when I entered, speaking with Poseidon."

"Poseidon is here? He rarely ever leaves the ocean."

Hades shrugged, a strange reaction for the God of the Underworld. "I do not know. I guess it is a family affair."

Ciro hugged him again and continued his search for his brother. He finally located the God of War in deep conversation with a woman he didn't recognize.

"Ares," he greeted. "You rang?"

The muscular man with flowing black hair and dangerous eyes whirled around and a smile broke across his face. Even though Hera was not pleased with Ciro's existence, Ares and Hades always welcomed Ciro with open arms. Ciro waved and Ares excused himself from his conversation and walked over to Ciro.

Ares patted Ciro on the shoulder then bowed his head slightly to meet Ciro's eyes. "I meant to speak with you about this before," Ares began, "but nothing here ever goes as planned. Then add the wars the people of this world seem to be bring against each other and that leaves Adrestia and I super busy."

"It is okay. What's wrong?"

"I heard about your fight with Gala. I am sorry you had to kill him."

"So am I. He used to be a good Shiver. Then something happened and suddenly I did not recognize him anymore. It is uncertain what transpired."

"It had to be the power. The humans have a saying, 'absolute power corrupts absolutely'."

Ciro eyed his brother with a raised eyebrow. "I see. Anyway, he posed an unnecessary risk to Terra. Mother was beginning to get warnings from Gaia. How did things get so out of control? *When* did things get so out of control?"

"I know not, brother. Perhaps it was while we were sleeping."

"Another human saying?"

Ares smirked. "Something like that."

"I could not allow him to continue his needless destruction." Ciro rubbed his eyes. "Damn, I have not gotten a wink of sleep."

"Well, in that case, I really hate to be the bearer of bad news but this has to be said. You and I need to have a discussion."

A small smile cracked Ciro's lips. "Whenever you say that line, I know something is very wrong. What is the matter?"

Ares turned toward the large gates leading to the Celestial Gardens dedicated to the fates. Ciro followed and once they were outside in the beautiful surrounds, Ares turned and spoke. "It is about Aerios."

A lump suddenly formed in Ciro's throat. Whenever that name cropped up, it was always preceded by danger, doom that had been slowly simmering over the past four hundred years. From time to time, Aerios would pop up, cause some natural disaster then vanish before anyone could get close to him. Deep down, Ciro knew Aerios was baiting him, testing his resolve while showing Ciro how smart he was. It was a humbling thing to know someone was going to do something horrible yet he didn't know when or how to stop it.

Ciro swallowed and nodded numbly, waiting for the horror to be unveiled.

"He seems to be out of control once more. He just caused a windstorm in the Sahara. It killed seventeen people, five of them children. Normally, I would not be worried, but we both know Aerios is never up to any good, especially when he disappears for six months then shows up out of the blue. To make matters worse, he then hammered it with rain—more rain than the place has seen in the past forty-five years. The people are furious. We know this is a small scale for him and whenever he does something like this it always leads to—"

"Something bigger. I know." Ciro nodded again. "I will have a word with him. I have not heard of any plots and Sisqo has not found anything, either. But lately I have been having this feeling as if I am being watched."

"That was probably him."

"Or Sisqo is right and I am just being paranoid."

Ares chuckled. "What is it the humans say? Just because you are paranoid does not mean they are not out to get you? He is rather secretive, which is what I am afraid of. When you wish to find him, he is nowhere and when you wish him gone, he is everywhere. He is so much like a child—when he gets too quiet go and find him for he is up to something, and chances are it's either painting the dog's toenails or lighting fires under the bed. Be careful. If you need me and Osaki, we will be there."

"And Adrestia, no doubt."

Ares chuckled. "But of course. It isn't a war if my beloved daughter isn't there."

"Touché. Thanks for this."

"You be careful."

With a smile and a hug, Ciro vanished once more.

* * * *

He spent the next few days trying to find his brother, but it was the ultimate lesson in futility. He searched all the usual places with no luck. When Aerios didn't want to be found—which was most of the time—he remained lost. When he did want to be found, there was always destruction leading right back to him.

"I am not certain what else we can do," Osaki said, leaning back in the chair and crossing his legs atop the center table. "We have spent the better part of the last few days searching for a ghost."

"Yeah," Ciro replied. "Do you think I should go and see Mother? Perhaps she would know where I can find him."

"I am not sure that is wise," Osaki reminded him. "I know she gave you her blessings but I do not think she wants to be an instrument in this war."

"She may not have a choice." Ciro got up to grab a couple of bottles of juice from the fridge. He loved the way the grape tasted. "I will just have to show her that leaving Aerios free is worse than having him dead— again."

"All this destruction by them for no reason," Osaki pointed out. "I do not get it. I want them to answer the same nagging question that has been plaguing me for years now — why do this?"

"You will not get an answer to that, my friend."

"I guess. I found that man you wanted me to look for," Osaki pulled something from the pocket of his luxurious kimono and placed it on the table. "But I must ask this."

Ciro sat and picked up the piece of paper. "What?"

"Is now the best time to look for your mate? I mean, now, when Aerios is so out of control — when he is obviously up to mischief?"

"I have thought of that."

"What is the conclusion you have reached?"

"I cannot stop thinking of this man. I have tasted him, Osaki. I know the couture of his body, the smell of his flesh… I need him."

Osaki nodded. "If you think he is the one Aphrodite has spoken of, then by all means. But I am still a bit confused as to why the oracle was wrong."

"I have been wondering about that as well. But my heart and body craves this human, so that has to mean the oracle was not correct."

"Are you not concerned by this?"

Ciro nodded. "I am. But there is nothing I can do about it right this moment. I cannot leave to tend to the oracle, so I will see what happens." He looked at the paper Osaki gave him and arched an eyebrow. "He is an architect?"

Osaki nodded and rose. "I must get back to Olympus. I feel my powers beginning to wane."

"That still happens? I thought they fixed that."

"No. That is the downside of being given a special pass into Olympus. My powers weaken the longer I stay away from it. There is no way of fixing it—that is the fine print they do not warn you about."

Ciro stood and hugged his friend. "Thanks again for the help."

"Any time, my friend. I will call if I need help," Ciro promised. "Right now, I must find Carter."

Osaki nodded, stepped away with a slight bow and vanished.

Ciro looked at the piece of paper in his hand once more, memorized the address then shoved it into his pants pocket. He picked up his coat and, while shrugging into it, made his way out of the door.

He tried figuring out a way to explain how he knew where Carter worked but as he reappeared outside and jogged up the large front steps, he had nothing. Carter Olabasu Architecture adorned the outside of the building, looking quite lovely with a rather elegant logo. A security guard's desk sat to the far right of the brightly lit lobby. Pictures from unnamed painters hung off the pristine silver walls, and designer light fixtures were suspended from the high ceiling. Ciro was impressed. Carter Olabasu had good taste and was obviously wealthy.

He stopped at the security desk as per a sign in the center and leaned over the counter. "I'm here to see Carter Olabasu."

"Your name?"

"Ciro."

"Hold on." The officer picked up a phone and dialed. "Hey, Carter—I got a man here to see you. Says his name is Ciro...uh-huh...sure thing." The officer stopped to laugh at something said to him on the other end. "Will do. And if you keep that up, we'll both be out of a job...okay, talk soon."

When he hung up and faced Ciro once more, he nodded then motioned to the large glass doors straight across from him. "Go ahead. I'll buzz you through. Go to the twentieth floor and it's to the right just out of the elevator."

Ciro was tempted to tell the guard he didn't have to be *let* into anywhere but remembered his powers were to be kept from humans. "Thanks."

He allowed himself to be buzzed in then followed the instructions. A smiling woman—one with a fake smile—greeted him then ushered him into Carter's office. The moment he entered, Carter stood and motioned for him to a seat.

"Deidre, please hold all my calls," Carter said in a voice that said all business.

"Yes, Mr O."

Ciro smiled at that. It may not seem like much to anyone else but it said Carter wasn't only boss, he was a *beloved* boss.

He turned and watched the door until it clicked closed. Falling into the chair, he stared at the dark-skinned man and tilted his head. Was it possible he'd gotten sexier over the few days he hadn't seen him? Then again, the first time he'd lain eyes on the man it had been in a dark club with music blaring and women grabbing his ass.

Carter sat and faced him. "How'd you find me?"

"Would you believe Google?" Ciro asked. When Carter tilted his head, Ciro chuckled and shook his head. "It wasn't like it was hard. Your name is on the outside of the building. I just had to ask around."

"Yeah, right."

"Well, there is only one Carter Olabasu in the phone book," Ciro lied, crossing his legs before him. "I just took a chance, hoping it was you. You are shocked."

"Truthfully? Yes. I mean, I didn't know you were that interested. Normally, these things end in passing flirtations then we both leave Firewall and go back to life as though we never met."

Ciro smiled and uncrossed his legs. He leaned forward and rested his elbows on his knees, meeting Carter's eyes. "Trust me—I am *very* interested. Can I take you out for lunch?"

Carter eyed the pile of folders on his desk. "Er."

"If Mohammed cannot go to the mountain, I must bring the mountain to Mohammed."

"You would bring me lunch?"

"I would bring you anything, Carter," Ciro admitted. "Now, what do you want to eat?"

A smirk tugged at the corners of Carter's lips. "That, my friend, is *very* a loaded question. But I feel a need for Greek today."

Ciro nodded and stood, desperately trying to hide his knowing smile "Give me about twenty-five minutes."

Carter shook his head but he couldn't help a smile. He tried getting back to work but just couldn't concentrate. Instead, he walked to the window, folded his arms and stared out. The view of the city was breathtaking. Each time he looked, he couldn't help thinking how perfect the choice was to put his office in that corner of the building. It wasn't overly flooded with sunlight when the sun was high but cast the perfect amount of light and shade. He continued enjoying the view outside. It was part city, part water. When he wanted to hammer out a thought, he stared at the buildings around him, most of which he'd designed and his brother had sold. When he wanted peace and quiet, he turned to the water. Many decisions had been made staring out at that view.

His mind drifted back to Ciro. He couldn't remember the last time a man had been interested enough to look him up for personal reasons. All the others had wanted something—money, sex, a break into the architectural world. Something told him it was still early for Ciro to ask for anything but he had a good feeling about this one. He chuckled, feeling silly. There was no way he could know anything about Ciro—they had only met for a grand total of a few minutes. He couldn't allow the fact Ciro was just so damn sexy have all the bearing on what happened next—even if all he wanted to do was crawl over that desk and tackle his fine self to the floor.

The ringing telephone jarred him from his thoughts. He inhaled deeply and took a step toward his desk to grab it. "Hello, Olabasu?"

"Hello, baby brother," Kofi greeted him. "I have a long lunch today and wanted to know if you would like to be my date. I'm buying."

Carter laughed. "I would love to. But I may have a lunch date."

"Lunch date? I didn't know you were dating anyone?"

"I'm not. Remember that guy from the club?"

Kofi cleared his throat. "The one who bought you the drink?"

"Yeah. Well he tracked me down, asked me out to lunch, but my desk is covered in paperwork so he offered to bring me back whatever I want."

"And what did you say?"

"I wanted Greek."

Kofi laughed. "Is he Greek?"

Carter blushed. "Yes," he replied sheepishly.

"Well." Kofi chuckled. "Enjoy your Greek. Call me later tonight? I really feel like dirt, the way we left things that night."

"Don't worry about it, Kof. I'm over it."

"Just, call me later? Okay? Let's have a beer together or something. Even if you're over it, I'll feel better just seeing you."

"All right. I'll call you the moment I get home and take a shower. We can figure out what's going to happen then, good?"

"Awesome. I love you, Carter. I know I don't say it much, especially after you came out. I just kind of assumed you knew and you didn't need to hear it anymore."

"I do need to hear it. That was the worst part of it, you know? Thinking you no longer —"

"But I do," Kofi interrupted. "Love you, I mean."

Carter's heart soared. He smiled. "I know, Kofi. And I adore you too."

No other words passed between them. Then there was the distinct click of the line disconnecting. For a moment, he held the phone against his forehead, wondering what just happened between him and his brother. It was true they'd replaced 'I love you' with 'see you later' or something equally as sterile, but the seriousness of what had just happened between them left him a little jittery. It felt like saying goodbye, but Carter knew better.

A soft wind blew across his face. He couldn't figure out where it came from. The windows to his office didn't open for they were up too high. They were just glass panes that allowed the sunlight in, beautiful and efficient. Still, he felt like he was standing outside and the gentle wind was caressing him in ways he'd never experienced or felt before.

Carter finally dropped the phone into the cradle and returned to his position by the window. He didn't realize how long he'd been standing there until he felt someone enter his office. Carter turned around to find Ciro smirking at him with an armload of bags.

"Where were you just now?" Ciro asked, walking forward. "I tried calling your name but you didn't answer. I was just going to poke you."

Carter hurried around his desk to take two of the bags from Ciro. He set them down. "Close the door, would you?"

"All right."

"Just had a conversation with my brother, and I was thinking," he admitted, before peering into a bag. "Is that Galatopita?"

"Yes. I got a few things because I did not know what you ate. Some men are picky eaters."

"You should come by my place when my brother Kofi and I are cooking. Nothing picky about it."

The two laughed.

"I was just going to say my men have to know how to eat." Ciro wiggled his brows.

Carter chuckled. "I see." He removed his jacket and rolled his sleeves up.

Ciro shrugged from his trench coat and tossed it over the back of a nearby chair. Together they sat and ate in relative silence.

That was until Carter couldn't take it anymore. He sighed and pushed a piece of chicken into his mouth before shoving his plate away and leveling his gaze on Ciro. "Tell me, what's a man like you doing single?"

"A man like me?"

"Yes—sexy, obviously successful—"

"You think I'm sexy? And how do you know I'm single?"

Carter made a face and reached for his plate again. "Answer my question first."

"I'm single because I've been looking for a specific type."

"You'll have to be a little more specific, Ciro."

"Handsome, smart, sexy — open minded."

Carter arched an eyebrow. "I see...and what do you think of me?"

"Well, I think you have most of those things. I know this is way out there, but does it say anything about me that all I have been thinking about doing since I walked into this room is tossing you across that desk and fucking you hard from behind while you yell my name?" He raised his shoulders then let them fall. "Aw hell, I probably should not have said that."

In the process of swallowing, Carter almost choked. His cock jerked to attention and began throbbing. He loved the idea of being manhandled by Ciro. But he had to be a gentleman — he had to think like an adult and not with his penis. He licked his lips, and suddenly it was becoming harder and harder to sit still. He bowed his head, silently stewing in his aching arousal.

"I am sorry. I *really* should not have said that," Ciro said softly.

"Ciro..."

"I know — it is too fast."

"That too. Look, we're both adults here. If we agree to it, there shouldn't be any problems. With that said, I'm not a slut. I don't just sleep with someone because he thinks I'm hot."

Ciro smiled. "And I do not expect you to. Honestly, sleeping with someone because they think you are hot is a horrible reason." He stopped speaking, chewed then continued, "I expect you to sleep with me because I have seduced you and you cannot live without me."

"I like that — sure of yourself. Ciro, the truth is that I would love to have you as a lover. But you have to understand that in today's world, I can't have you sleeping with others while you're with me. It probably sounds like I'm asking for a commitment but I..."

"I have no fear of commitments," Ciro interrupted. "I would have no need for others — I can tell you know how to please your man."

"And how can you tell that? By looking at me?"

For a moment, Ciro said nothing. He merely stared at Carter in a slow, heated way with a smirk on his lips. Carter trembled and hoped it wasn't visible.

"You could say that," Ciro replied, reaching for a napkin. "I can tell because of your mouth."

Carter touched his lips. "What's wrong with my mouth?"

"Nothing." Ciro smiled. "It is perfect — that is why. Anyway, I love it that you are a one-man kind of guy. And yes, I understand your worries about sleeping around. But we should take this slow — there are things in my world that you could never understand."

"Here we go," Carter said as he bit off a piece of chicken and chewed, staring at Ciro. "Look, I've heard it all before, so save it. Let's just enjoy the meal and then we can go on to being friends. That whole desk thing and the conversation before it didn't happen, okay?"

"Carter..."

"No — it's fine, really. I understand." Carter smiled.

"No, you do not understand."

Ciro walked over to hunch down before Carter. "Carter, listen to me. The moment I felt you, I knew I wanted you. I saw you and every part of me wanted to taste you — touch you, but my life is not something that I should bring someone into. But damn, I want you."

"Then why are you here?"

"Because I crave you. Lust is a confusing thing."

"I'm right here." Carter cradled Ciro's face. "Just reach out and touch me."

"I don't want to be selfish."

"Damn it, Ciro. I don't like games, so if this is one of those head games, you can leave the same way you came in and…"

Ciro snapped his head up and his gaze roamed to the window. He rose as though Carter hadn't spoken. Stiffly, he moved to the glass and stared out.

"No," he whispered. "Not now."

"You can't even focus." Carter pushed from the seat and walked up behind him. "We're trying to have a serious…"

He trailed off from there. Right outside his window, swirling violently and inching closer to the glass, was a tornado. Carter was more than confused but didn't have time to ask questions. Suddenly, the funnel made its way toward the building, and Ciro tackled him to the floor and covered Carter's body with his own. Carter's heart soared but crashed suddenly. The glass shattered inward, and he knew Ciro would get hurt. He struggled to get up, for he had to protect Ciro from the flying glass, but Ciro held him to the ground, shielding his body.

When the noise ended and Ciro let him up, Ciro dragged his hands over Carter's body. "Are you all right? *Please* tell me you're all right."

"I'm fine," Carter said. "You took care of that."

"Good." Ciro rushed back to the window and stared out. His hair blew about his face like a wild man's.

Something was wrong. By the time Carter pushed to his feet, Ciro had somehow gotten his coat off the back of the chair and had it on. He was stalking like a mad man toward the opening in the glass.

"Ciro! No! Stop! Please stop! It's a long way down!"

Ciro stopped and whipped his head back to look at him. Carter gasped softly and froze in his tracks. There was something cold and heartless in Ciro's eyes. Carter recognized it—raw, pure anger.

"Carter, it was an accident. The window has probably absorbed too much sun, that's all."

"No. There's something else and I will get to the bottom of it."

Carter took a step toward him, but a gust of wind stronger than any he'd ever felt shoved him over the desk. Carter grunted as he slammed into the ground with his left hand out. Pain surged through his arm and vibrated off his heart. He knew he couldn't stay down and wallow in the hurt he was experiencing. Moaning, he used the desk to help himself to his feet. When he stood, Ciro was gone.

"Son of a bitch, Ciro!"

A loud banging on the door shocked him but Carter ignored it. He rushed to the opening and stared out. There was nothing. The wind was strong but Ciro was nowhere to be seen. He glanced down, squinting to see if he could see Ciro's body on the ground. He was too far up to make out much of anything. People moved by like ants, furiously scurrying to and fro, as if there was nothing wrong. Carter hurried out of the office and darted past his worried secretary standing by the door.

"Carter, are you all right?"

"Fine," he managed as he jabbed the down button of the elevator. "Get someone to clean up the mess in my office and call the police."

"Sure."

The moment his secretary discovered the broken window, a loud, piercing scream echoed through the floor. Carter winced.

The elevator took forever to show up and by the time it got there, he was ready to burst. When he finally made his way down, he tore by security and flew outside. Broken glass lay everywhere. But there were no signs of blood, nor Ciro's body. Carter spun around, looking in every direction he could, fear penetrating his soul, driving him mad.

"Ciro! Ciro?"

How's this even possible?

He didn't reply, and Carter felt as if he'd lost something precious. His window was broken. He could deal with that with no problem for he had the money and the resources. But his body yearned for Ciro, and now he was gone from his life just as suddenly and mysteriously as he'd entered.

Chapter Six

It didn't take long for Carter to figure out that no matter how hard he tried or how long he stayed lying in bed, he wasn't going to get any sleep. He remained where he was, on his back, looking up at the ceiling. Ciro's eyes haunted him. First, they'd been filled with lust, a teasing mischief. Carter yearned for a man to look at him with such an expression. Then, like a snap of the fingers, the eyes had changed to such hatred and pain that he couldn't remember ever seeing the likes of it before. Was that meant for him? Did Ciro mean to show him that side? Then again, the window had smashed inward, casting broken glass everywhere. It was amazing neither of them had been hurt. That would cause Ciro some anger — wouldn't it?

Eventually, he shoved his feet out of bed and hauled on a pair of jeans and a graphic T-shirt. He stopped long enough to push his feet into a pair socks and runners then grabbed his keys and his cell phone. He had to get out of the house. For a bit, he sat in the car, gripping the steering wheel and staring out at the darkness around him. Nothing made much sense anymore. The windows in his office were shattered, which was completely insane, then Ciro had pulled a Houdini — *poof!* Gone.

At first, he found himself parked out front of his building with police tape everywhere. The cops didn't know about Ciro. How could he explain Ciro falling out of the window and not being there on the ground broken into a thousand little pieces? He couldn't find a way to tell them without being locked in a padded room in a straightjacket.

The police had gone through the scene and concluded they wouldn't take their investigation further since no one had been hurt and it was probably some kind of weird weather anomaly. With their promise to send someone to gather the police tapes the next day, everything was finished to his relief, but where the devil was Ciro?

He couldn't take the pain of not knowing anymore, and sitting outside the building where the mystery began was beginning to make him a little batty. After a few more minutes, Carter started the ignition and drove. Not sure where he was going, he merely took the streets and turns his mind suggested. Soon he was knocking on his brother's door in the middle of the night.

"Carter? What's wrong? Come in." Kofi grabbed his arm and led him through the house to the kitchen table.

Carter fell into a chair like a sack of potatoes dropped from an airplane.

"Here," Kofi said. "You look like you could use this more than me."

Carter turned and saw a glass of whiskey on the table. Normally he didn't drink the stuff. He hated the burning sensation it caused going down but with what had happened that day, he would try anything once to numb the confusion and ache he had inside him. Picking his drink up, he hesitated for a second then downed it. He had to press his eyes closed, as if it would stop the burn seeping down his throat to warm his insides. It didn't help.

"Tell me what happened."

"You haven't turned on your television today?"

Kofi shook his head. "I had a few things I had to get done for a deal I've been working on then I couldn't seem to put out the fires fast enough. Shit, I haven't had time to even scratch my butt, so I haven't gotten around to television. Why?"

"That guy from the club looked me up. Let's face it, I'm not that hard to find," Carter started, placing the glass back on the table before he gave into his urge to fling it at the far wall. "Like I told you when you called, he came and offered to take me to lunch. I couldn't leave so he brought the food to me. We were just talking about life, love, sex—those kinds of things. Then all of a sudden he got this look in his eyes."

"What look?"

"Like he knew something was about to happen—something bad. I was asking him a question then it was like I wasn't even speaking. He turned, as though he was going to look through the window. There was this sound...this crash..." He had to stop and hang his head as he again heard that awful, ripping noise like the roof was being torn off the building—*smash!* "The windows shattered inward and he went diving over the desk to cover me with his body..."

"Carter! Why didn't you call me?"

Carter tossed his hand up and shook his head. "Because I was fine and I knew you would freak out."

"This happened and you didn't call me?"

"No, because then, like I said, you'd freak the hell out—like you're doing right now."

"Of course I would freak out. Something like that happens in your office and I'm the last one to know? And how did that happened? I mean, that far up, the windows can't just break, can they?"

"No. Government mandates they be shatterproof. Hell, they're even bulletproof. The glass that high is like the glass floor in the CN Tower. You could run a truck over them and they wouldn't break."

"Spotty workmanship?"

"No. They were tested extensively when I put up that building."

"Then how do you explain them breaking?"

"I don't know. It makes no sense, right?" Carter dragged a hand over his head. "I've spent the last few hours just lying in bed wondering what in the hell happened. And I still have no clue." Carter pressed his lips into a thin line before speaking, "And that's not even the most stunning part. Ciro went right out the opening, Kofi—right out of it!—and when I went searching for his body, it wasn't there."

"What the hell you mean there was none? He couldn't have just vanished into thin air."

Carter swore under his breath and pushed the glass closer to Kofi, since he really did feel like throwing it. He lost more glass mugs and wine glasses that way. "I told you. He wasn't there. No body, nada, zilch, bub-kiss!"

"So what happened to his body?"

"Damned if I know."

Carter rose and walked to the kitchen window to look out into the perfectly manicured landscape behind his brother's house. He folded his arms across his chest, thinking back to the freak storms that had been hitting small towns around him. He wasn't quite sure why that came into his head but it did. Maybe it was just another freak storm. After all, the windows were made by humans—they were prone to error. Maybe it was just what it looked like, another big anomaly. Maybe when Ciro went to the glass a freak wind picked him up and carried him off—it could happen, right?

His eyes suddenly felt so tired. Carter bowed his head and rubbed his eyes.

"Carter, when was the last time you slept?"

"I don't remember. I tried falling asleep earlier but I just kept reliving that whole thing over in my head. No matter how many times I tell myself there's a reasonable explanation for all of this and try closing my eyes, here comes the nightmares. It went from questioning whether I could see myself growing something meaningful with this guy, to feeling aroused with his body atop mine, followed by absolute horror and dread. I think I have whiplash from it all."

His brother walked up behind Carter and wrapped his arms around him. He turned in Kofi's arms, pressing his face into his brother's shoulder, feeling more exhausted than he had in a long time.

"Maybe you should lie down for a little," Kofi suggested. "I hate seeing you like this and you definitely shouldn't be driving."

"I won't be able to fall asleep."

"Then don't sleep. Just lie there. I'll do some searching for this Ciro...what'd you say his last name was?"

"Pyktis. Ciro Pyktis."

"Okay. I have some friends down at the station. I'll call in a few favors and see what we can come up with. I'm sure he has family, and if he's missing, they will want to know."

"What are we going to tell them? 'Oh, I'm sorry, but I think your son, brother, uncle, husband is dead but we're not sure'."

"We have to start somewhere. Now, don't argue with me." Kofi pulled Carter from the chair, turned him toward the door and patted him on the butt as though a mom would her son. "To bed, now."

* * * *

Ciro walked across the sky as a swirl of wind led the way and streaks of lightning followed. He knew he was invisible to humans, but not to his brother who threatened to destroy his life. Regardless, his destruction wasn't what angered Ciro. What riled him terribly was the fact that Aerios had endangered Carter. That was one sin that could not be forgiven — ever. He was going to get his hand on the insolent jerk and burn his world to the ground. His eyes flashed lightning and his hair danced in a wind generated by his temper. He extended a hand out to his side and a small, silver shaft appeared between his fingers. Clenching his fist around it, it elongated into a staff with a lightning bolt on the end. It glowed golden then turned to blue. The top of the lance fizzled with charge, ready to fire.

"Come on out, Aerios," he thundered. "I am tired of these little games you seem to enjoy playing. Face your destruction."

"You are in love, dear brother." Aerios' voice echoed off the clouds. "We warned you against that, but I see you did not listen. You just had to fall for a human. Silly little Shiver."

Reeling in his anger, Ciro stopped and steadied himself. He was more powerful than Aerios. He knew that. But with his emotions dancing through him, he was allowing his feelings for Carter to cloud his mind. He inhaled deeply, held the breath before exhaling long and loud. He watched trees beneath him sway with his exhalation. Again, he repeated the action and looked into the air. Once he was sure his mind was clear, he lifted his weapon, swirled it above his head and fired.

"Not today, big brother," Aerios teased. He appeared in front of Ciro.

The smile on his face irritated Ciro to no end but he stood ready, waiting. "Brother or not, go after Carter again and I will end you."

"Promises, promises."

Aerios disappeared without warning. Ciro's anger surged. A bolt of lightning rushed from his body, fell through the clouds and split a tree in half. He had to stop and hold his breath, for he could feel the makings of a twister building in his veins. Aerios was just trying to rile him so he would lose control and cause a major storm. Ciro had to remember that fact the next time he fought Aerios, Ciro could destroy the very beings he'd spent his life protecting.

How was he going to explain it all to Carter? Before Aerios had attacked, Ciro had been certain he was strong enough to catch anything the rogue Shivers could throw at him. He was determined to protect his lifemate and succeed. He was sure he'd figured out how to get around the supernatural bullshit he was positive would begin happening around a human lover. But with each passing day, it was as if the rogues were chipping away at his resolve, and he hated that feeling. Not only that... He now had to decide if he should tell Carter the truth.

How would he explain walking on air out of that window?

The moment his feet touched the ground again, Ciro was off through the darkness to find him. He discovered Carter standing shirtless near a window with his arms folded across his chest. In the moonlight, Carter was beautiful. Ciro loved the way the rays flowed over Carter's flesh, giving it a hardened softness. But there was so much more about Carter that turned him on and tugged sweetly at his heart—from the way he leaned against the window frame, to the smooth darkness of his skin. It left Ciro feeling that if they ever made love, the world would implode around them.

A cool breeze swirled about him and he closed his eyes. The tree he leaned against took the brunt of his weight for his knees suddenly buckled beneath him.

Ciro felt like a freak, a stalker watching the handsome man from the darkness. He couldn't help himself. Bowing his head, Ciro tried desperately to breathe, to remember Carter was human and would never understand what was happening. How could he look into Carter's wonderful, big, brown eyes and tell Carter that he, Ciro, wasn't even human? How betrayed would Carter feel?

"I need you, Carter," he whispered. "I..." The other words died in his throat.

Carter's head snapped up and he pressed closer to the window. It was as if he'd heard Ciro's words.

I'm over here, Carter.

"Where?" Carter yelled. His voice echoed off the trees around them and Ciro knew for sure Carter heard him.

You are him. You are…

Ciro knew what getting involved with Carter meant—constant danger for Carter. How could he, in good conscience, allow that, especially when he was getting so much weaker and Aerios was becoming a bigger pain in the ass? Taking a deep breath, he slipped further into the darkness and made his way home. The instant he got there, he felt someone and knew Sisqo waited for him.

The moment Ciro walked in, Sisqo was sitting in the living room and immediately set in with asking questions.

"Where have you been?" Sisqo wanted to know, following Ciro into the kitchen. "I heard Aerios attacked. Did anyone get hurt? Why isn't he dead? Did he tell you why he's such a giant ass?"

Ciro didn't answer any of the questions. He dumped some whiskey into a glass, appreciating what humans saw in the liquid, and tossed it back. He tossed back two more glasses before turning his attention to Sisqo. "Once again, Aerios has managed to wreck my life. I am tired of it. If he wants a war then that is what I will give him."

"What happened?"

"When the Oracle Gnóseis told me my one true love was not a woman but a man, do you understand how absolutely mortified I was? To think I could lay with a man the way I had been lying with women all my life was…challenging, at best. But the oracle has never been wrong. She was right about that, so of course she would be right about a demigod being my true mate."

"Ciro?"

"She told me he would be a demigod—one who will love me for all my eternity. Still, I went through my life searching and searching, wondering which demigod Gnóseis was referring to. Then Aphrodite said it wasn't a demigod but a human. I knew one of them had to be wrong. Then I felt him. Just one scent and my whole world crashed in on me. I want him in ways that confuse me. I searched for my love—sure, it wasn't that long of a search after she told me. I found him. I thought about him tonight and he heard me."

"What? Ciro, if he heard you, then that means..."

"I know what it means." Ciro knew he was irritated with the wrong person but he just couldn't stop the rage from pouring out. "Eros wasn't playing a practical joke on me after all—Gnóseis was wrong. And now, my brother—my dear, wonderful brother—decided he was going to spend his entire existence torturing me. For three hundred years I have searched for this man until finally, there he was. Then there he went." He chugged another glass of alcohol.

"You found him? Where?"

"He was at the Firewall. The moment he walked into the room, I knew he was there. Long before I even saw him, I smelled him, I felt him, and it was marvelous. Today I went to have lunch with him and when I saw the exhaustion of games in his eyes, how could I have told him who I truly am? All I wanted to do was love him and hold him and my brother—" Ciro let out a painful growl and hurled the glass across the room. "The man who is supposed to be my protector, my shield against the world and the gods, against all those who sought to do me harm, takes it upon himself to go after him, to break my heart in the only way that could never heal again. My own *brother*."

"You must be certain before you start a war with Aerios."

Ciro swung to face his friend and walked toward him until he could feel Sisqo's breath against his face.

"Before *I* start a war with Aerios? Oh no, my friend. That ship has long sailed. Aerios started this battle a long time ago. I was perfectly happy to let him go on throwing his little tantrums. But he is not going to quit, and I cannot let him go after Carter again."

"So his name is Carter. You have not told me much of this man — in fact you have not told me anything at all."

"It is not important." Ciro backed away and picked up the bottle of whiskey. He stared at it before taking a long drink.

"Obviously it is. You cannot ignore this man — he is what the fates have woven for you. And to top it all off, Aerios has taken a liking to him. No one wants that."

"I cannot keep falling for him, Sisqo. I can no longer entertain the idea of being with him." He glared at the bottle of alcohol. All he felt after drinking the crap was worse. His head throbbed more, his knees weakened and his throat burned. "This stuff does not work. I do not see why humans consume so much of it. It does nothing for the ache."

"That is why there are programs for people who overindulge in alcohol, Ciro. You cannot drink too much of it."

After lowering the bottle to the counter, he turned to walk out of the room.

"Ciro."

He stopped and looked over his shoulder.

"You do know that if you need assistance with this, I will be there. I cannot see you break like this and do nothing."

A smile crossed Ciro's face. "I know, my friend. But some roads a man must walk alone."

"Are you forgetting, Shiver? You are no man."

Ciro nodded and exited the room. But he didn't gain the silence to ponder, as he'd hoped. There, sitting on his bed, was Hera.

"Oh what fresh hell is this?" Ciro muttered.

He shook his head and leaned against the doorframe, watching the woman who had hated his mother so deeply that she'd turned all his mother's offspring into monsters. Her black hair was flawless. It cradled a lovely face with eyes colder than the coldest weather he could create. She had a body to die for and that was probably what happened to anyone, other than Zeus, whoever touched her. They ended up dead.

"Why are you here?"

"I heard you have fallen in love," she said simply.

"I see. So I guess you are here to wallow in my heartache. If that is the case, Step-mother, you can leave the same way you arrived here."

Walking farther into the room, he stripped off his jacket then peeled off his shirt.

"You have grown into a rather sexy, young Shiver, Ciro," Hera cooed, floating up behind him and running a hand over his shoulder then down to the center of his back. Ciro arched away in disgust and whirled around to face her. Lightning snapped across the sky outside as a gust of wind imploded the window in the room. "Do *not* touch me!" He growled.

"Oh!" Hera shivered visibly.

It wasn't the reaction Ciro had been expecting. He wanted to scare her half to death but he should have known better. His roughness only aroused her—he could smell it.

"This one has fire."

"Why are you here?"

"I am here because, well...I may be of some assistance."

"You ruined my mother's life, took away my birthright and the inheritance of my brothers, and now you want to help me? I would not take it if you were the last goddess on Mount Olympus. Now go to Tartarus."

"Hell—Hades would not like that. What I would rather do is stay right here—" She lay out on the bed with a come-hither look.

Ciro walked closer to the bed and kneeled between her legs. Curling his hands into fists, he braced them on either side of her head. Leaning in closer, he lowered his mouth to her ear and lifted a hand to her face as his weapon appeared. It was a long lance shaped like a lightning bolt, sharp enough to take off a god's or goddess' head.

He pressed it against her flesh and took great pleasure in her surprised gasp. "Let me make a few things perfectly clear. I want *nothing* from you. I have never asked you for anything. I do not even like you. Come near my mother or me again, and you will regret it. Now get out."

She nodded jerkily. When he released her, she vanished and so did his weapon. Taking a breath, he pushed off the bed and strode to the chest. He'd just taken a seat and began peeling off his watch when Sisqo yelled his name from downstairs.

"Can I get no peace?" he thundered, pulling the door open.

But the moment he walked to the balcony prepared to holler at Sisqo, his words died in his throat. "Carter?"

"Hey—we need to talk."

"How'd you find me?" Ciro questioned.

Carter shrugged. "Would you believe Google?"

Ciro knew it was a lie but swallowed nervously. He'd called in a few favors and had had his house removed from Google Earth so that meant Carter's riches brought connections in high places. Even with that thought, he was still nervous as he descended the stairs slowly until he was face to face with his very heart. Hearing Carter's heartbeat was as if he was watching his very own soul pulse before his eyes. He titled his head, staring into Carter's gaze, wondering why Carter had searched for him.

"I will go out on patrol," Sisqo said, clearing his throat. "Ciro, call if you need anything."

"Take Adrestia with you," Ciro shouted, without taking his eyes off Carter. He didn't want to look away because he was sure Carter would disappear.

"Sure," Sisqo replied.

Ciro waited until he heard Sisqo's footsteps disappear, the door closed and the rev of a motorcycle engine outside before he stepped away. "Would you like a drink?"

"No—I just need some answers."

Chapter Seven

Carter could not believe the house when he'd pulled up before it. It was grand to say the least, with vines growing on the outside like some haunted mansion from a movie. When Kofi's friend at the station had come back with the address, Carter had thought for sure there was some mistake. Sure, he'd pegged Ciro as wealthy by the way he dressed. But the house before him spoke of old money. Fear rose within him. Suddenly he didn't feel as though he should be there. He meant to turn back but something kept him going, and seeing Ciro standing before him, shirtless and oh-so-sexy, made his long ride there and any discomfort he felt worth it.

"What happened at my office?"

"About that—I will pay for the damages." Ciro walked off into the kitchen. Carter followed him.

"Forget that. I'm an architect, Ciro. I can handle it. How did you get out the window without dying?"

"I think you should sit," Ciro said, climbing onto a stool. "This is something you should hear, because as much as it breaks my heart to tell you, it now involves you."

Kofi always told Carter growing up that he asked too many questions—that one day Carter would regret being so nosy. In that one instant, with those few words from Ciro, Carter was beginning to regret asking for answers. It was too late to turn back. He knew that.

Nodding, he sat across from Ciro. "Okay—go ahead."

"I knew I should have stayed away from you, but I just could not help myself. You smelled so good and I just wanted to taste every inch of you, hold on to you for as long as I could, but I was being selfish."

"There's that word again. Ciro, just come out and say it, damn it."

"I have pulled you into a familial battle that has been taking place for hundreds of years, and I am very sorry..." He stared at Carter for a while then licked his lips. "I am what you call a Shiver."

"Say what now?"

"My father is Zeus."

Carter arched an eyebrow then held up his hands while easing from the stool. "If you're not going to take this seriously, Ciro, then don't bother. Zeus? Jesus H Christ, what is wrong with you?"

Ciro grabbed him. "Please...how else do you think I got out that hole in the glass? What kind of wind do you think would have enough power to break through or blow you over a desk? You cannot break that window by smashing a fist into—hell, windows up that high cannot be broken by a chair being smashed into them. You know that."

Carter bowed his head and bit his lower lip, silently praying for patience. Lifting his head again, he exhaled and looked at Ciro. There was a sad plea in his eyes and, for the love of him, Carter couldn't figure out why Ciro's eyes drew him the way they did.

"This was a bad idea." Carter stood. "Shit, sometimes I think I'm the neediest motherfucker on the planet. I mean, come on. Let's be honest here. Any other guy pulled this shit on me I would be so fucking pissed off—but you—what is it about you that keeps me standing here putting up with this crap?"

Ciro looked up at him, shook his head and vanished. Carter looked around, wildly. He closed his eyes. That couldn't have happened. A man couldn't just disappear into thin air. But when he looked again, Ciro was still not there.

"Human beings have this knack to want everything in a neat, tidy bundle," Ciro said.

He still wasn't visible, and Carter's heart was hammering inside his chest. How could he hear Ciro when he could not see him? Swinging this one way then the next, he wanted to scream. He stuck his hand out, hoping to feel Ciro—but nothing.

"Do you believe me now, Carter?"

Ciro's breath was hot against the back of Carter's neck. When he turned to look at Ciro, Carter was only fast enough to see Ciro disappear again.

"What else do I have to do to prove to you I am who I say I am—*what* I say I am?"

Once more, Ciro was behind him so Carter reached back, grabbed Ciro and turned to look at him. Ciro's eyes flashed lightning—honest to goodness lightning streaks. He stepped closer, cradling Ciro's face to meet his gaze.

"You're not human…"

Ciro smiled, but it didn't quite reach his beautiful eyes. He turned his head and kissed Carter's hand, sending a nice, warm shiver down Carter's spine.

"No. That is what I have been trying to explain to you."

"You're a god."

"Not that either."

"Then what are you?"

"I told you, Carter. I'm a Shiver."

Carter couldn't believe what he was hearing.

"My father has a nasty habit of mating with those he shouldn't," Ciro explained, breaking through Carter's thoughts. "It started out with him just transforming himself into what they thought was a human male and mating with humans, then it escalated—nymphs, humans, demons. Nothing stopped him. Not even the fact he was married to the most manipulative, evil goddess of them all. Then he mated with my mother, the Goddess of the Storm Winds, and Hera finally got angry enough to do something about it. She cursed my mother's children, every single one of us. I was firstborn, so I got the brunt of it all. Ever since I was a child, I have been trying to protect others from my family."

"But you didn't turn out like the others—how come?"

"How come? Oh you mean why I do not thirst for world domination?"

Carter nodded.

"I know not. My brothers see humans as toys and expendables and I have been trying to fix that. But Aerios, the second brother to follow me, has been fighting me ever since he could walk."

"The second brother to follow you?"

"Yes. I was first to be born—followed by my brother Koi and then Aerios. Anyway, now…"

"He's set his sights on me. Why?"

"When Shivers hit the one-hundred-year-old mark," Ciro replied, "we have our futures read by Gnóseis, the Mount Olympian Oracle. Because I was first in my species, they read mine earlier than they should have, when I was but a child—ten years old. I cannot forget the look on her face when she saw me. She told me my one true love was to be half man, half god. I dated only a few human males from time to time, a few demigods but I just couldn't figure out whom Gnóseis was referring to. Then Aphrodite told me Gnóseis was wrong—that my true love was a human."

"So this oracle gave you the wrong information?"

"Gnóseis? I do not think she meant to."

"With all the people out there wanting to kill you, Ciro, how can you still see the good in this woman?"

Ciro shrugged. "I do not know. It is not that I am taking her side—she has caused so many hardships in my life. I didn't have time to develop when she had to do my reading. But Aerios has taken it upon himself to ruin my relationships but never has he actually put those men in danger. He just found other ways of getting rid of them—a haunt here, a lie there, hallucinations over there. When he crashed through your office window today, I knew Aphrodite was right. I knew for certain I had finally found you."

Carter swallowed and stood. He paced the floor a few times, silently, trying to digest what Ciro had told him. It sounded like something out of a movie, but Ciro was right. How else could he explain the window and Ciro getting out without getting hurt? There was something else there. That gust of wind that blew him over his desk was unlike anything he'd felt or heard of before. Then again, Ciro had vanished before his very eyes, not once but twice. There was no logical way to explain that and he wasn't seeing things. But did he really want to believe that some being jealous of his brother wanted him dead?

"So—your brother wants me dead to make you miserable for finding happiness all because your father couldn't keep it in his pants? What am I supposed to do now?" Before Ciro could answer, he was off and pacing again. Taking a breath, he stopped and spun to face Ciro. "I felt you a little earlier. Outside my window. I heard you tell me you were there. Was I hearing things? Did it happen because I wanted you so much?"

"I was saying goodbye."

"Goodbye?"

"I thought if I left you now, it would not be so hard later. Aerios would see that you weren't my true mate after all then you would be safe from my dysfunctional family."

"We're going to have to talk about this," Carter said softly. He was no fool. There was something happening around him and he just couldn't walk away. If this *thing* wanted him dead, the best place to be was with Ciro. Besides, Ciro was interested in him. He could see that as clear as he could see the nose on Ciro's face. "But not tonight—okay?"

"Can you stay the night?" Ciro asked. "I know I have no right to ask this after the trouble I have put you in. But please, can you stay?" He bowed his head with his hair spilling into his face. "Please stay with me."

Carter could still see his eyes flashing a light that should scare him. Still, Carter walked around the counter and stepped between Ciro's legs. He cradled

Ciro's face, staring into his eyes. He wasn't sure what he was looking for because he hadn't known Ciro very long, or for that matter, that well, but he needed to see something. Caressing Ciro's cheek, Carter allowed his eyes to drift closed, took a deep breath and brought his lips across to meet Ciro's.

One could tell so many things from a kiss. The taste of the kiss, the heat of the kiss, even the moistness, could give so many indications of what was between the two of them. He had to feel if there was anything more than physical attraction there. Playing this one by ear was out of the question. The throbbing in his chest had to be more than just wanting his dick sucked. It had to be something worth being in such danger for. When their tongues finally touched, a moan escaped Ciro, and it was as though Carter's whole soul burst into a sweet flame. Groaning, he wrapped his arms around Ciro's neck, catching the back of his head and pushing forward. Something jarred his heart, curled his toes and sent pleasure through his whole being. Finally, he managed to pull his mouth away and was shocked to see a gust of vapor leaving his lips when he exhaled, as though he was standing outside in the cold. Licking his lips, Carter inhaled and exhaled again, but the mist was gone. He looked at Ciro. The Shiver had his eyes closed, his pink tongue flowing over his lips, his neck stiff.

"Tell me what I need to do," Carter whispered.

"Your family?"

"My brother Kofi."

"We must protect him. Any way Aerios can hurt you, he will do it because he knows how much you mean to me."

"I can't mean *that* much to you."

"Carter—I have searched three hundred years for the man who was supposed to be my one true love. Aphrodite led me to you, and everything that has happened inside me and with my brother says she was right."

"How old are you, exactly?"

Ciro smirked. "Eight hundred and seventy-five. I know, I am very old and you are quite young and you may not want that but I…"

Carter choked and gasped. He reached a hand slowly down Ciro's body to massage his cock. It was hard under his hand, throbbing slightly. "I want to still be able to do this, get a perfect erection when I'm that old."

Laughing, Ciro said, "I can sense yours too. Do you want it sucked?"

Carter whimpered and pushed his hips forward. "Thought you'd never ask."

They didn't speak after that. Carter watched while Ciro slipped to his knees, gently eased Carter's cock from the confines of his pants and swallowed it. A low hiss escaped Carter's throat and his eyes rolled back in his head.

"Oh, baby…" Carter sighed.

Ciro merely moaned and sucked harder. Carter sank his nails into the Shiver's shoulders. He rode his hips upward, shoving his hard dick further into the back of Ciro's throat. Suddenly hot and cold air was washing over his arousal at the same time. It sent such desire coarsing through his veins, pulling with it his orgasm. Carter wasn't ready to come yet—he fought against it, curling his toes, biting his lips, even tugging at Ciro's hair. Nothing worked.

Then Ciro reached beneath Carter's shirt, took one of his nipples between his thumbs and forefingers and squeezed. All thoughts of control were gone and Carter watched through his passion-filled daze as he exploded against Ciro's lips and fingers.

"Come on, Carter," Ciro whispered. "Again…"

"I don't know if I have another in me," Carter panted.

"Only one way to find out, darling."

It shocked Carter when Ciro picked him up off the floor and placed him to sit on the counter. Carter watched as Ciro slowly stroked his cock in a tight fist. A cold sensation wrapped itself around the hard muscle. Carter groaned. It was as if an ice cube had passed over the tender, pinkish head of his dick.

"That feels so good," Carter gasped.

"You like that?" Ciro questioned.

"Oh, yes."

"Wait…it's about to get better."

With his lips slightly open in anticipation, Carter almost lost his mind as Ciro pulled the head of his dick into the hot wetness of his mouth. The cold swiftly vanished, leaving Carter hot and trembling. Carter always loved ice cubes against his skin but this feeling was so much better. When Ciro's tongue flowed over the head, the Shiver moaned before slurping noisily.

"Do you like that taste, Ciro?" Carter asked. His voice was husky, even to his own ears. But he couldn't dwell on the thought. His tender dick was inching further down Ciro's throat. Carter didn't have a choice as his hands gave out beneath him and he fell backward onto the counter. His eyes rolled back in pleasure and his toes curled as his legs twitched. "Oh, damn, Ciro."

Ciro feasted on him, licking the head and alternating between drawing Carter's dick down his throat and sucking on Carter's balls. Having those roll around in Ciro's mouth was new to Carter. No other lover had taken his balls into their mouth but it was mind-blowing, so damn good. He'd waited a long time but had never dreamed that one motion could cause him such pleasure. For a moment, he gripped the back of Ciro's head, keeping his mouth where he wanted it, having his tongue dance over those tender balls. When he was about to lose his mind, Carter released the back of his lover's head and dug his fingers into Ciro's hair. Now he wanted that hot mouth on his cock again. He pushed Ciro's head down to slide deeper in Ciro's throat. He gyrated his hips, loving the fire racing through his soul.

"Ciro…"

"Yes, my love." Ciro lifted his head, and their eyes met.

At that moment, Carter knew the touch stroking his thighs was familiar. It was as if he knew each touch, the burn behind each caress. "It feels as if we've made love before."

Ciro lifted him off the counter but trapped him there to take his lips. "We have," he whispered.

"But I would…" Carter trailed off in a gasp as Ciro spun him away from him and bent him over the counter. He yanked the rest of Carter's pants off and trailed a finger down Carter's crack.

"You would have remembered? You will again when I am through with you."

The roughness of his voice scared Carter but only for a moment. A beautiful breeze swirled through the room, leaving Carter feeling the same way he'd felt that night when he'd touched himself to thoughts of the wonderful man now standing behind him, inspecting his ass.

He couldn't help himself, sticking his ass out further, swaying his hips from side to side. Ciro kissed each of Carter's cheeks. His lips were hot. Carter sighed dreamily but the passion only stirred higher when Ciro's tongue slid over his skin.

"I am going to eat you, Carter," Ciro whispered, spreading Carter's cheeks. He licked it wet then blew against his hole.

"Oh, darling…" Carter whimpered.

"Do not be afraid to scream for me."

"Make me."

Chapter Eight

With a smile, Ciro basked in the first taste of Carter's most intimate area. He savored the taste against his tongue then let it slide over his lips. Groaning, he leaned forward and licked at Carter's hole, sucked it then flicked his tongue over it. His lover was delicious and he was certain he'd never be able to get enough. Ciro sank his tongue in then withdrew it, using it as he would his cock.

Tasting Carter was addictive, especially when Carter flowed, hot and tangy, over Ciro's tongue. He wanted more — needed to watch Carter's body tremble under his tongue again. Ciro met Carter's stare while gently stroking the architect's cock to life once more. He tightened his fist, gently shocking Carter with small bolts of lightning. Carter groaned and his head fell backward. Ciro loved the sight of Carter so turned on, so completely out of control. It turned Ciro on more than having any form of reciprocation.

"Oh!" Carter cried out.

Faster, harder, Ciro repeatedly shoved his long tongue in while slowly managing to strip. He dropped kisses against Carter's ebony cheeks but the tasty hole between those lush cheeks quickly called him back. The feelings dancing through him were foreign and amazing but he knew what they were. The same sensations Ares had told him about all those years ago were flooding his soul, driving him crazy and urging him toward climax. Slipping his mouth lower, he sucked on Carter's balls, playing them over his tongue before finding Carter's cock. Licking a trail upward again, he then plunged his tongue into Carter's ass.

"Ciro!"

A smirk danced over his lips and he eased Carter from the counter. Taking his hand, Ciro led him up the stairs to the bedroom then shoved him on the bed. He moved over Carter, kneeling between his legs. The drawer beside the bed seemed to open on its own with a gust of wind. A string of condoms and a tube of lube lifted in the air and fell to the mattress.

"Show off," Carter accused.

"You haven't seen anything yet." Ciro leaned in, taking Carter's lips.

So addictive.

He was completely dazed with the kiss. Each time he kissed Carter, he knew he could never give up on them. The more they kissed, the more Ciro knew his heart was meant for this man and no one else.

"We have made love before," Ciro repeated, pushing to his knees and trailing a finger over the familiar contours of Carter's body. "That night I saw you touching yourself," he whispered, dragging his finger down the thin line of hair that dipped into Carter's pubic area. "I knew I should have just walked away but I could not help myself. I yearned to feel you against me. I am sorry."

"The wind…"

"Again, I am sorry. I just wanted to touch you, and before I knew it, I could not seem to stop myself. I thought I was so strong but when it comes to you and the way you make me feel, I'm like a newborn baby — no control, no stopping it."

"Don't be." Carter sat up and caressed Ciro's face. "I never felt that good before. You did me a favor."

Ciro smiled and pushed him back to the bed. "Fuck me," he whispered. An intense glow filled his eyes. "I want it hard…deep."

"Isn't there a rule about fucking…?"

"Carter. I am a Shiver, remember?" Ciro smirked and reached for one of the condoms and a tube of lube. He gave them to Carter while twisting one of Carter's nipples with his free hand.

"Fuck," Carter swore, arching from the bed. "Dress me."

Carter watched as Ciro slipped the condom onto him.

"Bend over for me."

"What are you up to, Carter?"

Carter smiled and watched as Ciro crawled over on the bed and went up on all fours. He moved behind Ciro and spread his cheeks. Carter ran his tongue over his lips and bowed forward to lick. The Greek Adonis moaned, pushing his ass onto Carter's tongue. Leisurely, Carter ate at his lover like dessert. There was no hurry, for he wanted to remember, to feel and taste every inch of Ciro's delicious body. He enjoyed the tangy taste flowing over his tongue. Greedily, he groaned, sucking to pleasure his lover. Easing back, he inserted a finger, slowly pushing it in then pulling it out again. Ciro arched his back. Carter quickened the finger movement until Ciro's hole quivered.

It was time.

Slowly, he impaled Ciro and groaned as he let his head fall back. He couldn't move—not yet. He wanted to remember the first time he'd been engulfed in fire and held so tightly. He dragged a hand down Ciro's back, whispering his name before clutching his hips and driving deeper. Once he started, he just couldn't stop. From rolling his hips to driving in while clenching his teeth, Carter was in a fiery heaven that set every inch of his frame ablaze. He whimpered while his lungs screamed for air. His body was in control now. Everything he did was spurred by the lust and a deep desire to love the Shiver.

"Carter..."

Before he could reply, they lifted from the bed, and for a moment, fear charged through him. After only a second's hesitation, Carter's whole body relaxed and there was trust in Ciro he never though he could feel for anyone—especially a man who'd just confessed he was the son of Zeus. Still, he caressed Ciro's back to grip his shoulders and used that as leverage to slam harder and deeper into Ciro. Finally, Ciro's body stopped shivering. A cool burst of air charged through the room but Carter was too far gone to care. He couldn't stop the warm rush of climax that surged through him from the tips of his toes to make him shout with happiness. It was powerful and strong and tore from his cock, stopped only by the plastic of the condom. They slipped from the air and landed on the bed, panting for breath.

"I've never floated during sex before," Carter confessed.

Ciro laughed. "Sorry about that. You just make me lose myself when you touch me."

Chapter Nine

Ciro eased from the warmth of Carter's arms and hauled on a pair of track pants. When he entered the living room, Adrestia was sitting on the sofa, staring intently at the television screen. There were people arguing on the show about how they weren't the child's father. He smiled and sat beside her.

"How can you watch that crap?" Ciro asked.

"I am not sure," Adrestia said, tilting her head and sniffing the air.

"What do you smell?"

"You two made love," she said simply without taking her attention off the screen. "I can smell him on you. Are you sure that was wise?"

Of course he knew it wasn't smart. He took a breath and dragged a hand over his face. The frustration he felt in that moment made him angry. Why was it so hard to do something as simple as love? "I did not ask for any of this. I cannot go on living my life in fear and alone because my brothers are wayward hooligans."

"I know. But we are dealt certain cards. The humans are not the only ones given hard choices. This is one of those. You know now you must protect him and his family."

"Yes."

"I figured as much, so I have sent Hygeia to keep watch over your love's brother."

"Thank you. I was going to ask Hades to keep watch, but I think it's better Hygeia is there. I cannot run any longer, Adrestia. The war must end if I am to be happy or if Carter is to have his life back. Either way, I will not see him in pain."

Adrestia flipped off the television and turned her body on the sofa to pull a leg against it and under her butt. "Does he know what you are?"

"Yes."

"And yet he stays?"

"Yes."

"Good then. That is half the battle."

But Ciro wasn't so sure. When his brothers got it into their heads to cause trouble, it never got out again until something bad happened. Whether Carter stayed by his side was one thing but defeating Aerios could prove costly. He left Adrestia in the living room and made his way into the kitchen. He flipped on the coffeemaker then leaned his bare back to the counter. His mother had always wondered why he'd chosen to live among the humans, learning their ways of life and how to do things, but he found it comforting somehow. Living with the humans was not pretentious and everything was so much simpler. With humans love was love, lies were lies, hate was hate and truths were truths. Living on Olympus was a whole other headache altogether and he would not remain in the North Shores with his mother. That was her domain.

As the first drop of coffee hit the pot, he sensed Adrestia enter the room, so he turned to her. She looked concerned.

"What is it?"

"One of your brothers just breached Olympus," she said. "He was expelled and is heading here."

"Shit. Which one?"

"Guao."

"He is young," Ciro muttered, feeling as if the wind had been knocked out of his sails. Guao was one of his last brothers. He'd been hoping Guao was coming to help but he knew better. Aerios must have gotten to him if he'd tried breaching the protective shields into Olympus. He was the only Shiver, along with his brother Koi, allowed in. The others were all blocked.

"I shall meet him," Adrestia offered. "You see to Carter."

"See to me? What's going on? Who are you?"

Both spun to look at Carter, who was dressed only in his pants. Ciro took a breath. He hadn't felt Carter entering and that scared him. Obviously Adrestia was thinking the same thing, for her expression was one of perplexity. He took a breath and stepped toward Carter.

"I am Adrestia…"

Carter tilted his head and looked as though he was in deep thought. "My Greek mythology teachings are a little rusty—you are Ares' daughter?"

Adrestia nodded.

"Goddess of Misery and Revenge?" Carter asked.

"Something like that…"

"So, why are you here?" Carter pushed.

"One of my brothers is heading here. I must stop him before he gets to the house," Ciro replied before Adrestia did.

Carter instantly turned for the door but Ciro grabbed his arm.

"Wait one moment!" Ciro demanded. "Where are you going?"

"My brother…" Carter replied.

"Is being watched over," Ciro assured him. "I promise."

For a silent second, Carter stared into Ciro's eyes as if he was reading him then nodded. "Okay, then I'm coming with you."

"Carter, you…"

"You won't be able to persuade him otherwise, Ciro," Adrestia said, stepping forward. "We do not have much time to debate this. He shall travel with me. You get prepared. We shall leave the moment you are ready."

"This may get wet and cold," Ciro explained to Carter. "Put your shirt on."

After running from the room, he took the steps two at a time. He dressed quickly and called for Osaki. His friend appeared almost instantly in the bedroom, in full battle gear. He smiled. "I may need your assistance, my friend," Ciro told him.

"You do not have to explain. I was there to help get Guao from Olympus, but he escaped before we could restrain him."

"Carter is coming with us."

"Carter? The mate you've been seeking?"

Ciro nodded, and the two floated down the steps to stop in the kitchen where Adrestia, and Carter, now fully dressed, were waiting. None of them spoke but all of them turned for the door. Outside the plan was set. Carter would take his car and Osaki would go with him. Adrestia and Ciro would travel in their own way.

Ciro took a breath, kissed Carter deeply and, after caressing his cheek gently, he stepped back and followed Adrestia in disappearing. He was worried but Adrestia was right. There was no way he would have enough time to convince Carter to stay away. Still, taking a human into a battle with a bunch of super beings wasn't the greatest of ideas.

They all met at the spot he felt Guao's presence. "Stay in the car, Carter," Ciro pleaded. "If the fight comes toward you, I need you to get out and run."

"But..."

"Please...do this for me."

He saw hesitation in his lover's brown eyes but he smiled sadly and caressed the side of Ciro's face. For a moment, Ciro closed his eyes and basked in the closeness of this man he knew he would adore for the rest of eternity. Breathing was a chore for him so he turned his mouth to brush his lips over Carter's hand. The moment wasn't long enough, because the air changed.

Carter climbed into the car with Osaki and closed the door. Ciro kept his gaze on Carter even as he levitated beside Adrestia.

* * * *

It was hard to keep his mind on anything but what was happening. It started raining, lightly at first, one tap on the windshield, followed slowly by another until the sounds sped up in a symphony of water. Carter leaned forward to watch as the sky seemed to open and a funnel appeared falling hard and fast toward the ground. He covered his mouth, stifling a shout for Ciro to look out. To his shock, Ciro spun in the air, so fast the movement was almost a blur. Water deflected off his swirling coat as he fell backward suddenly and sent his foot upward, as though kicking a ball into a net over his head. A man, tall and slender fell toward the earth.

Before he got too far, Adrestia was on him, kneeing the man in the back, sending him flying upward.

"He is weakened," Osaki explained.

Carter spun around for a moment. He'd forgotten the Japanese man dressed like a samurai was in the vehicle with him. There was the loud clash of metal on metal and Carter jerked back to watch the fight above them. Both Ciro and the brother were now sparring with long blades. Each time they clanged together, sparks charged and sprayed around them. Ciro was knocked back, sending him sailing through the sky, crashing into the outside of a large building and slipping to the hard ground. Adrestia attacked. A gust of wind sent her flying through the air while Guao went after Ciro again. Ciro didn't move. He lay there, back propped against the wall and the rain pasting his hair over his face. Carter's heart fell. He gripped the door handle to shove it open, but Osaki grabbed him.

"Get up," Carter called. "Come on, Ciro...get up."

He slammed his fist into the dashboard, not because he wanted to but a single part of him thought Ciro would hear what he was saying or feel him. "Please..."

When Guao was close to Ciro, Carter saw Ciro stirring. The rain fell harder now, skewing his vision, so he turned on the car's auxiliary and flicked on the windshield wiper. It cleared the water-drenched glass in time for him to see Guao bending over Ciro then go flying back.

Carter eased in so his face was almost squished to the windshield to see Ciro slowly getting to his feet with a long lance in his hand as he began rising into the rain-filled sky.

"You are weak, Ciro," Guao called. "I thought you would have been stronger than this."

"Do you really want to see how strong I am, Guao? Then keep testing my patience." Ciro hissed. His voice was cold and scared Carter.

Carter couldn't believe that same voice had gotten rough and husky with desire mere hours before.

Guao turned to look down at the car, and Carter felt his breath catch in his throat. Was it time for him to scramble out and run?

Osaki must have known what he was thinking for the Samurai whispered, "Not yet."

"You brought him here, Ciro. Do you wish him for him to see your demise?" Guao taunted.

"No. I wish for him to see what a giant pain in my ass you are," Ciro countered.

The fight began again, both Shivers clashing and passing through the air as if they were the very wind. Everything moved at lightning speed. Adrestia was in the thick of things, two against one. Carter's eyes could barely keep up. Each time Guao attacked, Carter's heart lurched as if he was about to have a heart attack. Watching his lover in battle made him feel helpless.

"Come on," Carter whispered.

When they broke apart, the one falling was Guao. Adrestia flew as if out of thin air and pushed her blade forward, beheading Guao. The white of the rainwater, mixed with the yellow of what Carter believed to be Shiver blood and rained down on the earth. The head hitting the ground proved louder than anything Carter had ever heard. The sound was so bad he covered his ears with his hands and pressed his forehead into the dashboard. Still, he heard it when Guao's body crashed down with a sickening, wet *thwack*.

When Carter dared look, Adrestia was standing on the wet earth cloaked in saturated, red fabric, with her sword by her side, still dripping with rain and Guao's blood. Ciro hovered above the ground, holding his brother's headless body and looked up into the sky. Carter's heart broke even as he opened the door and rushed out into the rain. There was no imagining how it felt having to kill one's own brother. Yet, Ciro had to do it repeatedly. He didn't think that pain got any easier to deal with—Carter could tell. He stopped beside Adrestia and they both looked up into the heavens.

"Hera! This is on your hands," Ciro shouted. "He is my brother and I killed him."

Chapter Ten

The aftermath of the fight was unlike anything Carter had ever experienced. There was silence — an overwhelming quiet that followed. Everyone seemed to be in their own little world, even though Adrestia and Osaki stuck around. Carter wasn't sure what to do so he made them something to eat. No one ate much. He sat on the sofa with his legs over Ciro's while Osaki stood by the window, and Adrestia sat by the piano, staring longingly at the keys without touching them.

It was a while before Adrestia and Osaki disappeared and Carter finally managed to convince Ciro to climb the stairs to the bedroom. He sat on the side of the bed, gently caressing the hair from Ciro's face. Neither spoke — they hadn't said a word to each other since leaving the area where Ciro had to pronounce sentence over his brother's remains. Carter didn't understand it. However, it had broken Ciro in a way that was just heart-wrenching.

When he tried getting up, Ciro grabbed his arm. "I do not want to be alone."

"Oh, darling, I'm not leaving. I'm human and just need to pee."

That got a smile, however brief, to pass Ciro's beautiful lips. Inhaling, Carter kissed him quickly and Ciro released him. He hurriedly used the bathroom then climbed into bed with Ciro, pulling him close and rubbing his back.

"Please tell me you do not hate me for what I have done," Ciro whispered after a long silence. "I do not know how I can ask this of you but you cannot hate me."

"I don't hate you, Ciro. You had to do it."

"I must find my brother Koi."

"Why?"

"He is not evil, Carter. He is one of the good ones."

"How many brothers bent on world domination do you have?"

Ciro yawned and muttered something just before his eyes fluttered shut. Carter groaned and pulled the sheet up over Ciro's large frame. Carter stared into Ciro's face, feeling the Shiver's breath wash over his flesh. No matter how much he tried to sleep, Carter just couldn't look away. Slowly, he lifted a hand and dragged a finger down to the very tip of his nose.

"Baby..." Ciro sighed.

"I thought you were sleeping."

"I cannot sleep with you touching me like that—do you not know you turn me on?"

Ciro looked at him, and Carter gasped.

"You have the most beautiful eyes," Carter whispered. "It's always like you're gazing into me, past what you see to the parts I want to hide."

"I never want you to hide any part of you from me, Carter," Ciro replied softly. "If you cannot show me your flaws, then something is wrong."

Carter smiled and kissed the tip of Ciro's nose. "Just hold me and get some rest."

Ciro nodded and Carter moaned as Ciro wrapped strong arms around him. Ciro drifted off, and though Carter was comfortable and felt at home in Ciro's arms, he couldn't fall asleep. Each time he tried drifting off, he kept having this fear that one of Ciro's brothers would pop in and harm Ciro.

Each sound outside the window caught his attention. Carter spent the whole night, holding Ciro, having small conversations with him each time a nightmare woke him. At one point, Ciro's body began shimmering in and out of focus. He reached forward, sliding his hand down the front of Ciro's pants and massaged his cock to life. Ciro woke and his body went rigid once more.

Long before the morning arrived, Carter stood by the window staring out into the night, shirtless, with his arms folded over his chest. He'd tried calling Kofi and had spoken to his brother briefly, telling him to be extra careful. Kofi had thought he was overreacting but after some pleading, Carter had managed to draw a promise from his brother that he'd be cautious until the two could meet.

He was beginning to rethink not going to pick up Kofi. Ciro had insisted on going for his brother that night but Carter figured the less Kofi knew the better. Ciro didn't like that idea, so Carter had agreed to have Sisqo watch over Kofi secretly until the morning.

Inhaling deeply, he attempted to remember the last time he'd felt so loved—so absolutely, completely in love. He mentally ran through his recent relationships, the ones he'd actually thought would last. But he couldn't remember feeling so helpless with the joy that flowed through him at that moment. A shiver dashed its way through him and Carter smiled before turning to look at Ciro's sleeping form. Ciro's face lay turned to him with his dark, disheveled hair covering his eyes. The sheets had fallen to his waist, exposing a highly muscular shoulder and side. Carter smiled and walked to the bed. He sat with his back against the massive, elaborate headboard and stared at Ciro.

When he couldn't just look anymore, he caressed a hand over Ciro's face, brushing the hair away, then leaned in and pressed a kiss to Ciro's forehead.

"Are you all right?" Ciro asked sleepily. He shifted and lifted his head. "It is not light out yet."

"Was just thinking."

"Of what you have gotten yourself into?"

"Something like that. Your brother wants you to be miserable, and I'm not fool enough to think he won't start something especially with what happened earlier. It just pisses me off they would put you into this position of having to kill another one of your brothers. I mean—who does that? I don't understand how a brother with the same blood coursing through his veins could want you destroyed—I thought hate was only a human trait."

"The gods are petty, Carter. They, for the most part, live to realize only their needs and desires and to hell with everyone else. Aerios, on the other hand, is a special breed. He simply wants to have fun with humans and to do that, he must get me out of the way and once that happens, he can watch the world burn."

"That gives new meaning to sibling rivalry."

Ciro smiled.

"I think for a long while I tried not to fall for anyone," Carter explained. "I used my brother being uncomfortable with my sexuality as an excuse. The truth is, even if you'd come during that time in my life, I couldn't have resisted you."

"Shh..." Ciro whispered, sitting up and gathering Carter against his chest. "Do not think of this now."

"I can't help it. I feel I have to tell you everything that's boiling inside me, because he could hurt you — or worse. And what if it comes down to it and you have to kill him? He's your brother. I saw what killing Guao did to you. I can still see it in your eyes — it hurts you."

"If it comes down to it, there is no competition, no hesitation. I know what has to be done. Aerios poses a significant risk not only to you, but to this planet. I cannot allow him to spread his evil and I cannot allow him to harm you or anyone you love. It matters not what happens to me."

Carter pulled from Ciro's arms and jerked from the bed. He whirled to glare at the breathtaking man now sitting up in the bed and arched an eyebrow. "How can you say that? It doesn't matter? What am I supposed to do if he kills you? I feel this...this thing for you, this pull, and he could just rip you away like that without any hesitation, and you're telling me it doesn't matter if that happens?"

"If you are safe, no, it does not matter."

Turning to the window again, Carter stared out, trying to reel in the anger that flowed through his veins like a storm. He pressed his forehead to the cool glass and closed his eyes, just as lightning streaked across the heavens. He jerked away slightly when Ciro walked up behind him and pulled him against his chest. He stood there, head bowed, letting Ciro hold him silently.

"None of the others were worth spending my time to learn about. You — you are more than worthy and

I'm just getting to know you, Ciro. I can't lose you. I refuse to just sit here and let this ass just take you away!"

"I will do my best to stay with you, Carter. Please believe that. Please believe that I will fight to remain in your arms. But I would be a liar if I did not prepare you for the worst. I have waited for you, and it breaks my heart to know I may have to let you go. It is not easy for me either, Carter. Please understand."

Turning in his arms, Carter looked up, but Ciro's eyes were closed. His face looked tense and his lips trembled. The unbelievable pain written across his face was so evident Carter couldn't help the breaking of his own heart. He lifted a hand to caress Ciro's cheek to press his palm to the warm flesh there. When Ciro turned his head and kissed Carter's hand, all Carter could do was sigh and fall against Ciro's chest.

"This is insane, you know," Carter whispered. "This is completely and utterly insane."

Chapter Eleven

It took some doing but Carter finally managed a compromise with Ciro—he got back to his office with an escort. He didn't like being followed around by some guy with superpowers but what else was he going to do? His life had already been turned upside down by everything happening around him. Why should he let others with questions add to that? In the last two weeks, he'd taken more time off work than ever before and just knew someone would take notice if he kept missing days.

Carter stared out the replaced glass panes of his office. He hadn't dared enter it before they were finished. It looked as though nothing had happened—that a vengeful brother hadn't shattered the glass. And the man he was quickly falling in love with anything but a man. He folded his arms over his chest, turning his eyes downward, knowing Sisqo was lurking somewhere around there, just in case he was in trouble.

With a breath, he turned from the outside and allowed his gaze to roam his office. In a far corner, he saw a piece of broken glass. He hurried over and picked it up, turning it over in his palms, and was about to throw it in the garbage when someone knocked on the door.

"Yes?"

Kofi poked his head in before the rest of his body followed and his brother closed the door behind him. "So, er, don't freak out. Today I was at the office and something drew me to the window. Call it crazy or what, but I looked out and there was this guy. At first, I thought I was just being a bit nutty...but, well, er...I think I'm being followed. In fact, I *know* I'm being followed."

Carter made a face and walked to the window. He looked down, and the sun glinted off something. He inhaled. "Japanese man, dressed like a samurai?"

"Yeah. So I'm not going crazy." Kofi hurried to stand beside Carter and looked down.

"No. No you're not."

"Every time he's around, I know he is there because I get this feeling—it's this intense pull. I mean, I've never felt anything like it before."

"Almost like your heart is about to jump out of your chest, because it's beating so fast? Like someone injected you with adrenaline and you just can't turn it off? A feeling of heat pulsing through your veins, like you've inhaled fire and it's turning your insides into an amazing sunrise?"

"Yes...what is that?"

"I don't know." Ciro shrugged.

"And how'd you know it was him?"

"His name is Osaki."

"Er—what?"

"I think it's time I tell you what's been going on and I definitely believe you should probably sit down for this…"

Kofi stared at him for a bit then did as he suggested. Carter sat on the edge of his desk, fingers clasped and shoved between his knees. "Osaki is one of Ciro's friends. He's following you because you might be in danger."

"Seriously, baby brother, you are not making an inkling of sense."

"This is going to sound a little—or rather, a lot—far-fetched. Trust me. I know how it sounded until I got proof, but just hear me out. All of this started with Zeus."

"Zeus? The band or the hacker's program?"

"The Greek god."

"Okay? You lost me."

"Remember in high school when we were taught Hera was his wife and he slept with everyone but her? Well, it wasn't a lie."

"Carter…"

"Just let me finish. Ciro, the guy I met at Firewall, is Zeus' son. Zeus slept with the Goddess of the Storm Winds. They had a few sons, who Hera, in her anger, promptly put a curse on. Ciro is the first born, which makes him kind of a big deal and the others are out to kill him—well, some of the others are out to get him."

"That's a load of shit. First, there is no Goddess of the Storm Winds in Greek Mythology. There's Anemoi God of the Four Directional Winds, and that's it. Secondly…"

"Yes, of the four *directional* winds. Storm winds are stronger, more deadly. Trust me, there is a goddess of that and she is Ciro's mother." Carter eyed him. "Then how do you explain the samurai?"

"Some crazy Asian dude who thinks he's a samurai is not proof your boyfriend is a...god?"

"No, he's a Shiver."

"Look, I get that you have the hots for this guy and you want what he's telling you to be true, really. But who knows? Maybe the people stalking his ass, and now you and I, are mobsters—maybe he's into illegal stuff and he wants to scare you into not going to the police. Who knows with people these days? Maybe you just think he said all those things to you and you just need more sleep or something but..."

At that very moment, Ciro simply popped into the office out of thin air, cutting Kofi off in midsentence. Kofi shoved to his feet and Carter buried his face into his hands.

"How did you do that?" Kofi wanted to know.

"You did not tell him?" Ciro inquired. "My apologies. I did not mean just drop in. I did not know you had a guest."

"How...did you...do that?" Kofi repeated.

"I told you," Carter said, looking up from his hands. "He is not human. The Japanese man outside is your security detail."

"Okay, I'll bite for a second. Why do I need a security detail?"

"Because apparently Aphrodite claimed me to be Ciro's lifemate. Since his brothers hate him, they might try getting to Ciro through me..."

"And the best way to do that is to hurt someone you love," Kofi finished for Carter, who nodded. "Some family you've got."

"I am terribly sorry. I should not have gotten you into this mess."

"You're damn right you shouldn't have," Kofi snapped. "What am I supposed to do now? Walk around with a samurai trailing behind me for the rest of my life?"

"Not just the samurai," Ciro added. "We had Adrestia keeping an eye on you, and Hades for a little moment when Osaki had to go, then there was Sisqo."

"Oh." Kofi tossed up his hands dramatically. "Well, isn't that just fucking peachy? That just makes it *all* better, doesn't it? The God of the Underworld and the Goddess of Misery and Revenge are just the people a guy needs to hear are following him around!"

"Kofi, I understand…" Ciro began.

But Kofi whirled around and went nose to nose with the Shiver.

"No, you don't understand shit. If you'd only put my life in danger, I could understand—sort of—but you put my brother's life in this hell too and for that I cannot forgive you. So don't tell me you understand because if you knew just how fucking pissed off I am right now, you would *not* be here."

Carter hopped from the desk and stepped between the man he loved and the one he adored. "Okay you two," Carter told them, pushing at each of their chests. "We know this situation sucks but we're going to deal. Ciro, gimme a bit with my brother."

"Very well. Sisqo and Osaki will remain with you until Osaki has to return to Olympus. His powers get weaker the longer he remains here. Adrestia or Hygeia will take his place then."

Carter kissed him and he popped out. He stood, face away from his brother to inhale deeply then turned. "I'm sorry."

"You're sorry…" Kofi fell into a nearby chair and rubbed his hand over his mouth. "You're sorry. He's sorry. I'm sorry. We're all fucking sorry—and dead."

* * * *

After leaving Carter and Kofi, Ciro made his way to the North Shores. He rarely went there but desperate times, as the humans say, had caused him to visit twice in the past little while. Taking a breath, he peeled his coat off his shoulders and felt when his mother entered the room. He turned to look at her and saw just how exhausted she was. He offered her a smile.

"Hello, Mother."

"Ciro." She rushed forward, fell into his chest and kissed his cheek. "I am sorry for Guao."

"Mother. Why do you apologize each time this happens?"

"Because it is my fault. I should have just said no," Thýella replied. "Now my sons are terrorizing the people I care for so desperately and I have not the heart to stop them. I never once thought of what this could be doing to you."

"It is my job to protect you, Mother."

"No." Thýella shook her head vehemently. "I am your mother. It should be my duty to protect you. You are my child but I have failed you all. What mother allows her children to run amok in the world slaughtering one another, stealing one another's happiness? I knew allowing Zeus to bed me was wrong but he was so powerful and beautiful. Now I shall pay for these indiscretions with the lives of my babies..." She touched Ciro's face. "Why can my children not be happy with the power they have? Use this curse of Hera's for good, like you? Why do they wish to see everything destroyed?"

"I do not think that is what they are doing, Mother. They want ultimate power over earth."

"But that is Gaia's domain."

"Yes. But what they also fail to realize is if all of them want power over the humans, the humans will fight back. If the humans lose, my brothers will still not be satisfied for then they will fight amongst one another and, once the smoke clears, my dear brothers will be kings of nothing."

Thýella sobbed silently, pressing her face into Ciro's chest.

"I have fallen in love, Mother."

She looked up into his face then. "Koi told me your love is human."

"Yes. And he and his brother are in danger. His brother, Kofi, hates me now because all this is my fault. With my selfish wants and desires I put their lives in peril and I do not know if they will ever be able to forgive me."

"You will make this all better," Thýella told him, patting him against the shoulder. "And it will be all right again—better even."

"Mother."

The voice caused Ciro to swing around for the doors to the great hall.

"Peace, my son. It is but Koi."

Ciro took a breath but rose from where he sat. Thýella walked to the door to greet her second oldest son with a hug. Ciro shook Koi's hand, and Thýella excused herself so they could talk. They walked from the great hall and along a corridor with arched windows exposing the vast garden.

Ciro folded his arms behind his back, "Has Aerios returned here?"

"No. He would not dare," Koi replied, his gray eyes flashing anger. "I am not certain what his problem is. I have been meaning to speak with you about your lifemate, this human."

"What about him?"

"When you told me he was human I was surprised because we were all told your life mate was male and a demigod. Something is amiss here. That cannot be right."

"He is *the* one, Koi. I feel such a pull to him that baffles me. He hears my thoughts and feels me. Aerios is after him, Koi, which means Aphrodite was correct and Oracle Gnóseis was wrong."

"Oracle Gnóóseis is never wrong. There has to be something to all of this. I will look into it. In the meantime, I will get the rest of our brothers together and we can figure out what to do next. Sending someone to get into Olympus means one thing. Aerios is up to something and I am quite certain whatever that *something* is will be mega big."

"Mega? Since when have you been using such terms?"

Koi laughed. "Since I have fallen in love with this little dark-skinned child that makes me laugh more than I think I should. We have to stop Aerios, Ciro, or he will destroy all the happiness I have found on earth."

Ciro nodded. "Very well."

"I will get to Oracle Gnóóseis and the others. While I am away, I think you will have some explaining to do..."

"How do you know...?" In that moment, he could hear Carter calling for him. He groaned.

"Did they not tell you? If your life mate is human, after the first time you bed your human when he calls for you, you will be able to hear."

"Yeah, they never explain the fine print," Ciro replied cheekily.

"You move fast, brother. You have already bedded him. I must congratulate you."

Ciro chuckled, "You are speaking of this like it is some kind of match. He is my mate and I cannot seem to resist him."

Koi shrugged. "Correct me if I am wrong, brother, but the whole deal of being in love, of having a lifemate, is for you not to be able to resist each other, right?"

"I have to go," Ciro replied and hugged his brother. "Let me know what you find and tell mother I had to go but I shall return."

"I shall," Koi promised. "But this conversation is not over."

"Oh, trust me, baby brother, it so is." Ciro said over his shoulder and laughed. He beamed himself back into the great hall to get his coat and even as he was shrugging into it, he disappeared.

Chapter Twelve

Being home again was strange. He wasn't alone. Normally the only other person in his house was his brother but now, Sisqo stood in his den staring out of the window at something in particular. Shrugging, Carter left the room and climbed the stairs to his bedroom. Since it had been argued that being with Ciro was safer, he began packing a few things to take back to his lover's place. Once that was finished, he grabbed the bag and made his way back down the stairs. His stomach growled and he tried remembering the last time he ate.

He couldn't.

"I'm going to make something to eat," Carter explained to Sisqo. "You want anything?"

"No, thank you."

The two entered the kitchen, and while Sisqo sat at the island, he set about creating a sandwich to carry, as well as a fruit platter. He hadn't had a chance to work out in the last little while so he probably should eat healthy. "So tell me, are you a Shiver too?"

"No. I am a demigod."

"That means you're half god, half human—" Carter racked his brain going through his Greek gods and their children. "Who's your father?"

"Poseidon."

"Oh, like Percy Jackson."

Sisqo laughed softly. It was the first time Carter had seen that look on his face. "Yeah, something like that."

"Do you eat?"

Sisqo nodded. "I assure you, I eat. It's just...I'm not hungry at the moment."

Their conversation was slow at first but after a few getting-to-know-you questions, they were talking as if they had been friends for years. Carter needed that, for he didn't have any friends aside from his brother and a few business associates that had taken off to Aspen for a big golf tournament. Golf wasn't his game on the best of days. He couldn't see it as a sport anyway.

"Sometimes I envy humans," Sisqo admitted, popping a grape into his mouth. "You have this...this air about you that I could never have. I think you call it freedom."

"What do you mean?"

"Well, the gods are petty. They go to war over the simplest things. My father was just recently allowed back into Olympus for something he had no control over. So we're constantly looking over our shoulders to see if one of our parent's enemies or one of Ciro's brothers will freak the hell out and come after us. No freedom there."

"Yeah. That would suck."

"Come on. We should head back to Ciro's."

Carter picked up the bag with his sandwich to eat in the car and stopped to grab some juice while Sisqo got the bag he'd packed earlier with his clothes. They drove silently away from the house and that gave Carter some time to think of everything happening in his world.

"I'm scared I'll have to let Ciro go to protect my brother."

"He wouldn't hold that against you," Sisqo replied. "I know he would want you to be safe and happy and if that is without him, he would let you go."

"It's not that easy, Sisqo. I have never felt anything like what I have for Ciro. It would kill me to have to let him go before I can explore — but my brother is in danger now. I can't let what my heart wants overshadow my love for him and his safety."

"There are some decisions…"

Something heavy crashed into the hood of Carter's car, causing him to swerve. The wheels squealed. The vehicle careened to the side and though he tried pulling to a stop, he just couldn't manage it before it slammed into a light pole. The airbags deployed but Sisqo stuck his hand out across Carter's chest, keeping him stiff against the back of his seat. Dazed from the crash, Carter heard the fizz of something beneath the car. Sisqo was already out and pulling him from the damaged vehicle.

"What was that?" Carter questioned, sitting up and rubbing the back of his neck.

They both turned to see a man, dressed in gray, walking toward them with a sword in one hand.

"Son of a bitch," Carter swore.

"You must call Ciro."

"What are you going to do?" Carter asked, thinking of Ciro.

"Hold him off. You get out of here."

"I'm not leaving you!"

"That wasn't up for debate, Carter. You are my cousin's heart and I am not having it ripped from his chest. Go."

Carter slipped over the small ravine and hit the dusty floor hard. Leaves crinkled beneath the weight of his body. The distinct clash of sword on sword echoed through the air as he was pushing to his feet. There was no way he could leave Sisqo to fight this guy alone. Even if he had no powers, he had to do something until help could arrive.

He dug his feet and fingers into the dirt and climbed his way back up to the road. He hunched low, watching what was happening. The assailant could fly, so he seemed to have an advantage over Sisqo. Ciro's cousin took a hit to the side of his head and sailed across the space into the wrecked car.

There was only one thing to do.

"Hey!" Carter stood and waved his arms above his head. "I'm the one you're after, right? Here I am."

"Carter! What are you doing?" Sisqo called. He rose but only succeeded in falling back to the ground in a heap.

The attacker turned in Carter's direction, sending his heart racing. The man shoved a hand out toward Carter and he felt himself lifted off the ground. Struggling didn't seem to help. If anything, the choking feel at his throat grew worse.

"So, you are the one Ciro chose," the man spat, levitating. "Aerios believed you to be untouchable. That was a joke to me. I can merely crush you beneath my thumb like the insignificant insect you are."

Carter coughed. He could barely breathe. He struggled harder, kicking forward, trying to get the man to let him go. He rose higher into the air now. Something caught his attention at the corner of his eye and he tried desperately not to turn to it, just in case it was help.

Suddenly his ascent stopped, his attacker lay on the ground and Sisqo stood over him, blade out. That caused Carter to hit the ground again with a grunt. He coughed, sputtered as he tried sucking air in.

"I told you to go," Sisqo stressed.

"And leave you alone?" Carter sputtered. "Never."

Sisqo made a sound in his throat before turning toward the being, blade up for an attack. There was a sickening gargling sound just as Ciro appeared to Carter's left side.

"Sisqo, stop," Ciro called, rushing to the fallen man's side. He fell to his knees beside him. "I do not know you. Who are you?"

"But I know you..." The attacker gurgled.

"You are not Shiver. I cannot feel your essence," Ciro pushed.

"Who cares what he is?" Sisqo snapped. "He is trouble. He works with the rogue Shivers and he has to die. Either that or you must pronounce sentence over him."

"No," Ciro replied, standing. "I will allow mother to deal with this one."

"No," the being on the floor begged. "Please. I'd rather die than face Thýella again."

"Not to worry." Ciro eyed him. "You will get your wish—at least a part of it anyway. Can you see to Carter getting back to my place?"

Sisqo nodded.

"I shall return as soon as I can..." He stopped, walked closer to Carter and cradled his face. "I am so sorry...please forgive me."

"Go. We'll talk later."

* * * *

Ciro dropped Carter's attacker on the ground by his mother's feet and stepped back. "Do you know who this is?"

"Yes…" Thýella replied, walking around the shaking man on the ground. "His name is Aceplese. He was the one who betrayed me the night I conceived the Shivers. He was the one who brought Zeus to my hiding place. I told you I would see you again, Aceplese. Now you are a thorn in my son's side." Thýella faced Ciro again. "Has he told you who sent him?"

"No. Not yet."

"You are going to cooperate, are you not, Aceplese?" Thýella focused on Aceplese once more. "You will tell my son what he needs to know then you and I are going to spend some private time together."

"She said nothing about any of this," Aceplese stuttered. "I was only supposed to kill the human and walk away."

"And what was your reward?" Thýella questioned. "Zeus already prized you with immortality. What more could there be?"

"Wealth…"

"Who sent you?" Ciro asked.

"The oracle—Gnóseis," Aceplese admitted then curled into a ball.

The bottom to Ciro's heart fell out and he merely stood there, shaking, eyes cast on the sniveling immortal on the ground before him. "You are a liar."

"Why would I lie?" Aceplese questioned, voice quivering. "There is no reason for me to keep up pretenses any longer."

"I must go, Mother," Ciro exclaimed.

"To your love, I assume."

"Yes."

"Very well, my son." She kissed his cheek. "You do that. I will go play with the toy you've brought me."

Chapter Thirteen

Carter woke up to Ciro nuzzling his neck. Gasping, he sat up to wrap his arms around Ciro's neck, hugging him tightly but wincing and groaning from where he'd hit the ground earlier. "You've been gone a while," Carter told him.

"I am sorry. I had to speak with my mother." Ciro kissed Carter deeply. "She misses me and sometimes our visits run longer than normal."

"You weren't gone too long."

Ciro eased back and turned on the bedside lamp. He caressed Carter's face then inspected his side and shoulder with a disapproving look on his face. "He hurt you."

"I'm fine, Ciro. Really. Well, a little achy but fine."

"It is swollen." Ciro dragged a tender fingertip along the bruise.

Carter gasped. Even such a gentle touch hurt.

"I will take a bath tomorrow and it'll go away," Carter promised.

Ciro said nothing. He merely eased Carter back against the bed, crawled over him and fused their lips together. Heat radiated from both their bodies and Carter couldn't help how turned on he was. All the questions he had in his head about the attack were gone the instant their tongues touched, setting off a firework of pleasure surging through him.

All his life he'd searched for a man who made him feel precisely the way he was, now that he had all those beautiful sensations pulsing through him, Carter knew he couldn't let that go. He'd never find that with anyone else. Ciro nipped at Carter's nipple.

"Damn..." he muttered.

He lifted as if he had no control over his body. Each spot Ciro's mouth touched was as if he was slowly going to explode. He tangled his fingers in Ciro's hair but the Shiver merely took that hand and passed his lips over every finger then kissed the palm. He did the same to the other hand, lacing their fingers together, then pushed Carter's hand back to the bed. For that moment, they just stared at each other.

To Carter, the moment was just as intimate as if they were making out. Every inch of his body craved Ciro, wanting to be stroked by his long fingers. He rolled his hips upward, causing their cocks to collide. Ciro's eyes rolled back in his head as a low sound escaped his throat.

"You do these marvelous things to me," Ciro whispered.

"You're preaching to the choir."

Carter pushed Ciro's body up then slid down it against the bed. He happily took the Shiver's cock into his mouth and sucked on it slowly, lashing the head and shaft with his tongue. His reward was a nice, hot stream of pre-cum on his tongue. Ciro drove his hips down, sinking his dick deeper into the back of Carter's throat. It caused his eyes to water but soon he relaxed, allowing his lover to use his mouth in such a vulgar way, it made Carter blush. He enjoyed it and was almost disappointed when Ciro pulled back and shimmied down him to meet his eyes.

"Fuck me," Carter whispered softly. "Can you do that for me?"

Ciro smiled, an expression that sent Carter's cock twitching against his lover's body. "Turn over…"

He readily did as Ciro asked and without reservation. He pushed his ass up until he was on his knees, head against the bed and his cheeks spread. When a cool drop of lube fell against him, Carter moaned in pleasure and anticipation of this one man taking him, the one who made every part of Carter come alive with a simple touch.

Then he received what he was so desperately craving. Ciro's thick cock pushed against his hole to the tight sheath within. The first insertion was slow and Carter held his breath as his toes curled. But it didn't remain that way. Ciro gripped his hips, stood over him and fucked him hard, fast. Each push sent the Shiver's cock so deep, Carter didn't have a choice but to shout for his lover and tremble.

"Ciro…oh, damn. Ciro…"

In response, Ciro spun him around and drove into him again. This time, Carter's knees were braced against Ciro's firing hips, their gazes locked. Carter could tell when his lover was close. Ciro's eyes changed from their beautiful, fiery gray to all blue, glowing beautifully within the darkness of the room. The curtains gust forward with a distinct sound like a windstorm had taken up inside. Still, he didn't care. He clung to Ciro, their chests pressed tightly together, and allowed his climax to course through him a million miles per hour.

"Carter..." Ciro whispered, kissing the side of Carter's head, nibbling on his ear then dragging his mouth down to Carter's neck. "Good night, my darling."

"But you..."

"Will be fine. Please, go to sleep."

Carter was much too weak to complain but he made a mental note to do so in the morning. Ciro eased from him but didn't go far. He only pulled the sheets over both their bodies and cradled Carter gently. Carter closed his eyes, muttering something his brain was much too fuzzy to decipher.

* * * *

Ciro lay awake staring at the ceiling long after Carter had fallen asleep again. Carter's fears were still sitting on his heart, tugging at him. He understood them fully. He'd spent an eternity waiting for a lover to be so overly concerned for him, for that showed love. Finally, he'd found it, but walls were closing in on him, threatening to destroy that blissful peace he'd discovered with Carter. Aerios was a sore that had become infected, and now he had to deal with it or be swallowed whole by his brother's rage and stupidity.

The hours ticked by. Still the sun was nowhere to be seen. Eventually, he closed his eyes for they were too tired to remain open, though he had no expectations of sleep. The next time Ciro opened his eyes, however, something poked his side. Jerking upward, he brought his hand around with the blade already manifested but frowned and made it disappear.

"Damn it, Ares," he whispered fiercely to his brother. He pulled his body from Carter's and ensured his lover was still asleep before getting off the bed. He stopped long enough to haul on a pair of pants then grabbed Ares' arm and yank him from the room and into the den. "Can we please keep the popping in and out to a minimum? Carter is cool with it but I don't want to push it."

"Sorry—did not have a choice. We need to have a conversation about our brother and it needs to be now."

Ciro rubbed his eyes and flopped into a nearby seat. Ares did the same, and for a moment, both simply sat in heavy silence. Neither of them were looking forward to the brash conversation that needed to happen. Ciro understood that. They both knew the consequences of that talk and Ciro was not sure he was ready for the outcome. Putting it off only made this worse, so Ciro leaned forward, braced his elbows on his knees and took a deep breath.

Ares was the first to break their silent pussyfooting around. "Your human, does he know?"

Ciro nodded. "I had to tell him after Aerios attacked at his office. I thought for sure he would run, but he's taking it remarkably well. His brother, on the other hand, not so much."

"So he knows what you are and, still, he remains?"

Ciro nodded again.

"Humans are very intriguing creatures. Their love can be so strong, yet they can be so volatile."

"I had Sisqo guarding Carter and they were attacked by an Olympian immortal."

"Say what? I thought your fight was only with the rogue Shivers."

"That was my thought as well but it seems someone else wants Carter dead. The instrument of their choosing was Aceplese."

"Aceplese? That sniveling little puke?"

"It seems everyone knew the guy but me. Either way, he did not look as though he had such connections but apparently looks can be deceiving."

"No," Ares replied. "But he sells his services to the highest bidder. It makes him worse."

Ciro inhaled and nodded. "I gathered that after I brought him before Mother. It turns out Aceplese was the one who told Zeus of Mother's location. She tried hiding from his advances. To keep me from leaving him with Mother, he told us who sent him to harm Carter."

"Who?"

"Oracle Gnóseis."

Ares surged up from where he was sitting and shook his head. "No. That cannot be correct. Can you trust his word? I mean, there is nothing else about him we can take at face value."

"We would all tell the truth if we thought it would save our lives. Something has been happening with Gnóseis and this may just be the thing. You have to admit...she has not actually been straightforward with me, and now this?"

They fell silent again. Ares returned to his seat with his fingers gripping his long hair against his scalp. "I must get to the bottom of this. First Gnóseis was wrong about your predictions—does that mean she has been wrong about everything? And since she's never wrong then it would mean she lied...but to what outcome?"

"I know not, brother. But we can figure that out another day. Why did you visit?"

"Oh, right. Aerios just set off a storm over the Caribbean."

"But it is not storm season. The farmers wouldn't have been expecting one—this could destroy everything for them."

Ares smiled. "That I understand, brother. But Aerios cares not."

"Is he there now?"

"Yes."

"Then I must go. Please remain here and keep watch on Carter. I do not want any harm to come of him."

Ares nodded.

Ciro climbed the stairs and hauled on some clothes. He grabbed a few things and shoved them into his pockets. He meant to leave but he just couldn't without feeling Carter's flesh against him once more. He pressed a kiss to Carter's head. Instead of staying asleep, Carter moaned and looked up.

"You're dressed."

Ciro smiled. "Yes. I must go. My brother is causing pain once more and I have to stop him."

"I'll come with you. Just let me..." Carter was already halfway out of bed before Ciro managed to grab his arm.

"Not this time. I must go alone. It is in the Caribbean and since I cannot fly the human way, I must go without you. Ares will be here with you."

"Ares? As in the God of War?"

"He is also my brother." Ciro nodded. "Come. I can introduce you before I go."

Carter continued out of bed and got dressed before Ciro led him down the stairs.

Chapter Fourteen

Descending the stairs, Carter wondered how Kofi would take the rest of all of this. It was easier for him, since his heart was leading the way, but what of Kofi? He'd been so upset the last time they spoke. Carter was trying desperately to give him space but with this new development, he wasn't so sure space was the best of things. How was he going to explain Ares, the God of War?

Taking a breath, he smoothed a hand over his cornrows and licked his dry lips. He had to remind himself to take things once step at a time—fight one battle before beginning another. But even as he entered the den, Carter knew that was easier said than done. His mind wouldn't focus on simply one issue. It kept flashing all of them together in a tangled web in his head. With some difficulty, Carter managed to pull himself together long enough to notice the large, muscular man by the window. If he'd blinked, Carter probably would have missed him, for he was standing so still. It was as if he were a statue. He was dressed in all black except for a red band around his left wrist.

When he turned, Carter noticed dark eyes, a perfect face with long lashes and a proud nose. He stepped forward, his eyes focused on Carter even before Ciro spoke.

"Ares, please meet Carter Olabasu, and Carter, this is my brother, Ares."

Carter shook the god's hand, taking note of the strength in the shake.

"It is a pleasure, Carter." Ares bowed his head reverently.

"Likewise."

"Now I must go," Ciro said.

Carter wanted to hold on to Ciro, just to keep him there. Fear rose within him and he clutched Ciro's hand.

"It will be all right," Ciro whispered, as if reading Carter's mind. "Your eyes are filled with fear. If I require assistance, I shall call for it. Try not to worry. Why do you not bring Ares to Kofi and carry him back here? You and he will be safer within these walls."

Carter smiled and nodded. He expected Ciro to leave. Instead, he stepped to Carter, wrapped an arm around his hips and pulled him into his chest. Carter moaned and instinctively his eyes drifted shut. With a helpless whimper, Carter offered up his lips and sighed dreamily when Ciro kissed him. Their tongues flowed over each other's, drawing electricity through Carter's being. Finally, Ciro pulled away and Carter slumped into the seat behind him. He watched as Ciro took one final look at his brother then vanished. Carter held his breath to steady his racing heart and hormones, before turning to look at Ares.

"Shouldn't you be going with him?"

Ares smiled and sat across from Carter. He leaned in, leveling his gaze on Carter. "No. I am where he needs me to be, with his heart."

Carter closed his eyes and slumped back against the seat. "I don't get it. He may need help. No one can fight a war alone, you know? You're just going to let him go by himself? How is...? I don't understand."

"One thing you need to understand, Carter. Ciro may not be a god, per se, but he is very powerful. And what is it that you humans say? A man with everything to lose is quite dangerous?"

"Actually, it says a man with nothing to lose is dangerous...but I understand what you mean. So I guess now we wait..."

"Now we wait. But he gave us something to do. Let us go to your brother."

"I don't have a car..."

"Neither do I, but I get around." Ares shrugged. "Come, take my hand."

Carter eyed him. "This is not *A Christmas Carol.*"

Ares blinked at him. "Say *what* now?"

"Um...never mind." Carter was still uneasy for he'd seen all those movies and read those books. They all ended the same way when a supernatural character said something like 'touch my robe' or 'take my hand'. Carter wasn't sure he was ready to vanish in thin air and reappear somewhere else. That could not be natural for a human's body. "I'm human."

"I get that. Just, trust me, please?"

"Do you even know where my brother is?"

"Of course. What a question."

Carter shook his head and reached out for Ares' hand. The instant he took the god's fingers, something happened. There was no snap of fingers, wiggle of the nose, or comedic sound like *I Dream of Jeannie*, but he did vanish. It was as if he had a million tiny fingers caressing his body, pulling him one way then the next. It was strange and uncomfortable but did not last long. Before he knew it, he was standing outside Kofi's place.

"I thought it best we don't just pop in. I know all this was hard for you, so I can only imagine what your brother would say if we simply appear."

"Good call…" Carter agreed. He released Ares' hand and almost instantly, Osaki appeared at their side. Osaki shimmered like a television with bunny ears antenna. It was very strange to watch.

"I was wondering when you would be here," the samurai said, phasing from view for a few seconds before appearing once more. "I am very depleted. I must go back to Olympus."

"I'm so sorry," Carter said. "I forgot you were the one here. I thought Adrestia was with you…"

"She had to leave. I will be back the moment I am recharged."

Carter nodded and after hugging Osaki, he watched as his brother's guard disappeared. Rummaging through his pocket, he found Kofi's house key and let himself and Ares into the house. "Kofi?"

Nothing.

"Kof?"

"In the kitchen!"

Carter hurried down the corridor and stopped at the door, watching Kofi silently. His brother stood preparing a sandwich while the television on the counter played a game with the volume muted.

"I can't see him," Kofi spoke without looking up from his work. "But I know he's out there."

"Who?"

"The God of War. Who'd you think I was talking about?" Kofi snapped. "The Samurai. I don't feel him anymore but he was there — I know it."

"I was just going to say, I am right here, so I am not outside," Ares said, peeking over Carter's shoulder.

Carter tapped his forehead into the doorpost. "Kofi, meet Ares — Greek God of War."

"Great! We have an immortal Samurai, Shivers who pop in and out magically, so why not the Greek God of War?" Kofi muttered, twisting the cap back onto a bottle of mayonnaise. He then rested his side into the counter and eyed Carter. "What's going on now? Giant apes climbing skyscrapers in Tokyo?"

"We want to take you back to Ciro's place," Carter explained. "It's safer there."

"It is only until Ciro's battle with Aerios is over. After that, you can return here," Ares told him.

Kofi's shoulder rose and fell. "Can I talk to my brother — alone — please?"

Carter turned to glance at Ares, who nodded and exited the house. When he turned to Kofi again, his brother had this expression on his face that Carter knew all too well. Kofi was not impressed.

"Is this going to be what our lives will be like from now on?" Kofi demanded. "I have strange men following me around, popping out of thin air, me looking over my shoulders that one of your lover's psycho family members will come after me and you? Is this it? When I said I was good with you dating again, and dating men, this was totally not what I meant. I meant some lawyer from Boise who thinks you have a nice ass! This — this is insane!"

"I know that. Do you think I meant for any of this to happen?" Carter found himself getting irritated and slowly building into a full outrage. "Kofi, for fuck's sakes—I know you're upset but damn it, cut me some slack. I'm dealing with this the best way I know how. And you throwing a fucking tantrum is *not* fucking helping."

He stopped and tried to calm down but that didn't work. "You're not the only one pissed off about all of this. I am bloody furious. For the first time in years, I have a man who wants me, and not just for my money—no, he wants *me* and in a second it could all be gone." Carter swallowed the lump in his throat and brushed his stinging eyes with the back of his hand. When he spoke again, Carter's voice cracked. "Do you know what it feels like having to watch the man I adore fight with his brother? Do you have any clue what it feels like to have some wayward Olympic God wannabe come after me? Shit, I am dealing with this the best way I can."

"Well, you're fucking failing."

Carter growled and swung, slamming his fist into the nearest wall. It left a massive hole in it. "And you're not helping," he fired back.

"What do you want me to do? You're the one dating this *Shiver*. You should know how to deal with this!"

"Well shit. I should know how to deal with Greek gods and creatures invading my life, shouldn't I? Because this kind of fucking crap happens to me every day."

"There's no need for that."

"For what, Kofi? What the fuck do you want from me? You can walk away anytime you want. No one is holding a gun to your head making you stay. Shit man—I'll have Ciro figure this out with his brother then you can go."

"Don't say that. You know I'd never leave you."

"Then what? I'm supposed to stay here and put up with your accusations and asinine comments just because you feel some misguided sense of loyalty to me because I'm your brother? I don't need added pressure, not from rogue Shivers and definitely not from you."

"Carter..."

"No. I don't know how to handle this any more than you do and I'm trying here, but you just keep riding my ass — there is only so many times I can say I'm sorry and still mean it and right now I don't know if I give a shit. I came here because I know I brought you into this and I'm trying to keep you safe — if you wish to stay here, I will have to ask Ciro to send Hades or Adrestia to keep you company until we can figure it out with Aerios. So take your pick. You are starting to make my head hurt and I really don't need that right now."

Kofi frowned but his face softened some. "Fine...I'll come, but I don't like it."

"Noted."

Chapter Fifteen

Ciro stepped into being, hovering over Cuba. The storm was still raging but the center of it was high above him in the sky. It was as though it was just sitting there. Below him, trees swayed dangerously from side to side and zinc from roofs blew loose, tumbling around while other debris mingled in the dangerous air.

He could sense Aerios, but there was no sight of him.

"Show yourself!" Ciro called. "Let us get this over with."

Still Aerios stayed away, causing the storm to worsen. Frowning, Ciro held his hand down at his side and his lance appeared. It glistened in the rain.

"Ever since you were born, Aerios," Ciro called, hunting his brother, "you have been broken. It seems you left the factory floor that way and no amount of fixing will help you. Zeus knows I have tried, Aerios," he shouted to the now howling wind and drenching rain. "I have tried putting the fact you are my brother above my hatred for you."

"How touching," Aerios teased. "Like I said—I tried. But you've cured me of that horrible habit. It is so obvious my troubles will not end until I end you."

Aerios appeared before Ciro, weapon in hand, and lunged forward. Ciro eased out of the way of the slashing trident and appeared once more behind his brother. The rain worsened then, drenching them both and showing Aerios' growing wrath. Lightning and thunder followed closely as trees swayed to and fro beneath them. With Aerios' rage came more damage to Cuba. Buildings blew apart like paper in the rain. Vehicles danced in the wind, slamming into other cars or homes. Crops the Cuban people worked tirelessly with to make a living sailed around them in a twister of chaos and it all broke Ciro's heart.

Ciro's lance clashed with his brother's trident as he forced Aerios to rise higher and higher above the ground. Sparks from their weapons flew through the air for moments then died in the rain. He disarmed Aerios by crashing into his body and jerking the trident from his hand. It fell to the earth, spinning wildly. Sparing it a quick glance, he reached for the back of Aerios' neck and tugged. It seemed Aerios had expected that, for he easily slipped from the grip.

Ciro growled.

The wind around them picked up speed, knocking him off balance. Ciro stuck his arms out to steady himself and looked at the trees below him, hoping the storm would spare the country. The farmers depended on their crops for survival, and with a storm this early in the year, everything could be destroyed. Ciro's distraction allowed his brother to catch him off guard and Aerios' recovered trident sliced Ciro's arm. The pain caused him to shout his discomfort to the heavens, lose his concentration and fall through the clouds. He descended faster, out of control as he stared upward to see Aerios coming at him in a death dive.

Spreading his legs, Ciro managed to stop his fall and braced for impact. Aerios slammed into him and tangled together, their bodies sailed down toward the earth.

Pain shot through Ciro's back as he slammed into Pico Real del Turquino. The mountain seemed to crumble beneath the force of their weight. Aerios rose instantly, but Ciro, squirmed, his back arched in pain. His weapon disappeared, for he couldn't seem to focus to keep it in existence. The wind picked up speed, sending pieces of wet rock flying at his face, slicing through his flesh, tearing a hiss from his lips. But he couldn't remain where he was, wallowing in his discomfort, for Aerios was attacking again.

Ciro was too weak from both hits to react. He remembered his promise to Carter—he needed to keep his word, but his body was just not willing. Closing his eyes, he gritted his teeth and pushed for his lance to come back.

A howl of pain sounded above him and Ciro opened his eyes to see Aerios flying through the air. Hovering above him was Osaki, the Japanese Samurai warrior admitted into Olympus after his death for saving Ares' life.

"Carter said you could use some assistance, my friend," Osaki said, lowering beside Ciro. He helped Ciro up.

"I thought you went back to recharge."

"You should know it does not take long. Now let us finish this fight and get you home."

"Wait...his brother..."

"Is fine. Kofi agreed to stay at your place, though I hear it took some convincing. Focus now. My hit only stunned Aerios. We both know it will not remain that way for long."

Ciro nodded, gritted his teeth and lifted his hand. The weapon returned and shimmered slightly, for his mind was still a bit hazy.

"Pull it together, man," Osaki demanded. "*Kangaeru!* Think!"

Aerios was back. He moved toward Ciro, whose weapon still hadn't completely materialized. His head throbbed. He took another hit to the chest and fell across the land, taking out a few trees. He sat up, only to have Osaki land on top of him.

"Are you all right?" Ciro tried lifting Osaki's head. His friend merely groaned, twitched then passed out. Ciro laid him gently on the wet ground.

"Did you think he could protect you, Ciro?" Aerios hovered in the air above them with a smirk. "He is no god. He does not belong on Olympus. Now...be a good little Shiver and die so I may dispatch with your lover."

Flipping his head to clear his wet hair from his face, Ciro rolled out of the way of an attack to protect himself and Osaki. He pushed himself in the air. "The pathetic thing about your life, dear brother, is that you do not know what it feels like to be loved. Whether Osaki could protect me or not was not the point—the point is, he loves me enough to try."

"Love?" Aerios mocked. His laughter echoing off what mountains remained from their fight. "Love is a human emotion, for it makes you weak, Ciro. Shivers don't have that luxury. Love is a pathetic emotion humans use to ruin each other's lives."

"And yet, I once loved you," Ciro confessed.

Ciro didn't give Aerios time to collect himself—he attacked. The two tussled in the sky until Ciro's anger won out and he slammed an elbow into his brother's chest. Aerios landed atop some trees, flattening them. Everything moved fast. Lightning streaked across the heavens as their weapons clashed against each other, sending sparks sailing through the skies with rain and thunder. At one point, Ciro landed in a field of pumpkin, killing about three lines with the force his body hit them and slid across the space, but Ciro couldn't stop. His back collided with the base of a tree that split down the middle.

The lance he swung was stronger now, ready to taste blood. There was another round of fighting, and though Ciro should feel weak, the anger pulsing through him sustained him enough to hit Aerios long enough to slam him into the ground. Ciro surged from where he was and landed atop Aerios. The earth shook with the force of it. Though he wanted nothing more than to take Aerios' head back to Carter as proof he would now be safe, Ciro pressed his weapon hard against Aerios' neck.

"Do it. Kill me," Aerios demanded.

"I am *not* going to kill you," Ciro replied. "There are other ways to make you suffer without having to draw your soul from your body."

"I should have known—coward. You do not have it in you."

"Believe me, nothing would please me more than to kill you and give Hades a little more fun in his eternity. But I will spare your life for Carter. For some reason, he does not wish you death—mercy, another pesky little thing I adore about humans. But I assure you, brother, you will suffer like no other Shiver has ever suffered."

"What are you going to do?" Aerios struggled against the hold Ciro had on him.

Ciro clamped down harder, meeting his brother's eyes, and saw fear boiling within them. "Aerios, son of Zeus and Goddess of the Storm Winds, I now pronounce sentence over you."

Aerios fought harder. Ciro pressed his palm to Aerios' chest, causing a blue light to engulf his hand.

"No!" Aerios protested, struggling to get away. "You cannot mean...no. This is not fair."

"Fairness has nothing to do with it, Aerios. You crossed the line going after Carter. That comes with no forgiveness."

"But you cannot mean to do this."

"The same people you detest so dearly are now your sentence." Ciro said, lifting his hand higher until the light turned into a slow, spinning blue ball that hovered over Aerios' chest. "You have betrayed everything the Shivers stand for. You have threatened everything Mother fought to protect—the people she loves so desperately... For that, I make you what they are."

He pushed from Aerios' body, and the shimmering blue light rose slowly between his palms. Aerios screamed his displeasure but Ciro didn't care. The sky darkened. The rain and wind stopped and everything went silent. He pushed the light upward. With a growl of force, the ball shot into the air, cutting through the darkness with a low, rumbling sound. It finally hit the heavens and disappeared. A few seconds passed before the sky seemed to part and the light reappeared. Except this time, it was white. Ciro turned his head toward his fallen friend, Osaki, and the ball slid through the air and stopped above Osaki's body.

"Do not do this to me, Ciro!" Aerios pleaded. "You cannot give him my soul."

"I take no pleasure in your sentence," Ciro explained. "You are, after all, my brother, and I love you. But you have caused too much damage—too much sorrow. You have taken too much from me that I do not wish to part with. I cannot trust you to behave. I cannot trust you to leave my love alone. I have to teach you what mother should have when you were a child. Every action has a consequence, Aerios. You must be prepared, always, to deal with those consequences. And for now, this is your lesson. I will not lose my friend."

With that said, he used his powers to lower the bright, white light into Osaki's chest. Osaki coughed and stirred, while Aerios cried his displeasure, Ciro walked to Osaki's side and hunched down. "You have done well, my friend," Ciro said to Osaki. "And for that, I have given you new life."

"What have you done? I feel...I feel...different."

"You are now my brother, Osaki. You have inherited the spirit of the Shivers."

"You mean now I can..." Osaki lifted his hand above his head then dragged the hand to the right. A gust of wind left Osaki's body and the sky cleared. "I am now a Shiver."

"Yes."

"What's wrong with Aerios?"

"Aerios has been sentenced."

"To what?" Osaki arched an eyebrow.

"Humanity."

Chapter Sixteen

Carter sat on the balcony of Ciro's large house and hung his head as he waited for Kofi to speak. The silence was driving him crazy—not knowing what Kofi was thinking. But he didn't deserve to take this time for contemplation from Kofi. Having Ciro and the rest in his life had to be a lot for his brother to take in, and Carter would give him time. He knew his brother might be confused. First, it had been the news he was gay. Now, he had to explain that his lover was a form of god at war with his brother and that the Greek God of War and his fear-mongering daughter were sitting in the living room playing chess.

"It's too much. I know," Carter whispered. "I'm sorry to be doing this to you again."

Kofi chuckled then walked over and flopped into the seat beside Carter. "If I hadn't seen Ciro just appear out of nothing, I'd have thought I needed to get you some help."

Carter laughed. "Sorry about that."

"What exactly is Sisqo?"

Carter shrugged. "A demigod. He's Poseidon's son."

"Like Percy Jackson!"

Carter chuckled. "That's what I said. I'm sorry this hasn't been easy for you Kofi. I really am. I just... Please believe me that I'm trying."

"This whole thing has brought out some rather strange feelings in me—I'm not going to lie. They make me worry and just... I spend a lot of time at nights, lying in the dark wondering. Like Osaki, where did he come from? Aside from Japan but what exactly is he?"

"Well, he is what they call an Olympian Immortal."

"What does that even mean?"

Carter chuckled. "Not sure. I think it means he was given special entry into Olympus." Ciro took a breath and dragged a hand over his head. "But what I'm sure of is that Ciro loves me enough so I don't have to worry about any of this too hard."

"How do you know he loves you?"

Carter remembered the conversation they'd had before Ciro left and wondered how the fight with his brother was going. "This fight he went to—he said if he had to die to keep me safe he would."

Kofi's eyes widened. "He said that? But you just met."

"I get it, but there is something he said that just broke my heart."

"Well, don't keep me guessing—tell me."

"He said he had been looking for me for about three hundred years."

"Huh? How old is he?"

"Eight hundred and seventy-five."

Kofi whistled. "Damn. That gives new meaning to the term May-December relationship."

"You're a fruit. I feel something strong for him, and if he survives this, I want to try making it work with him. But..."

"Well...I just got used to you being gay. I'm pretty sure I can get used to you doing it with a man who can make our world implode."

Carter chuckled. "He won't make our world implode—just mine."

He glanced at Kofi, who stared back with a confused expression on his face. Carter wiggled his brows suggestively and Kofi burst out laughing.

"Oh wow," Kofi gasped through his mirth. "You're wrong for that."

Carter grinned. "Besides, he's one of the good guys."

"I just worry."

"I know..."

"Carter." Kofi took a breath. "I think I might be—"

"Carter! Kofi! Come quick!" Ares hollered from inside.

Carter jerked from his seat. All thoughts that Kofi wanted to say something else gone from his mind as he charged into the house with Kofi close behind. They hurried down the stairs and skidded to a stop in the living room. Ciro stood next to Osaki. A body floated in the air beside them. The moment Ciro saw Carter, he took one step forward and crumbled toward the floor. The floating man hit the floor, hard, but Carter didn't care. He rushed forward, caught Ciro in his arms and helped him into the sofa. Carter caressed the wet hair from Ciro's face and kissed his forehead.

"Come on, baby. Open your eyes," Carter whispered. "Please. You have to be okay."

"He fought a hard battle," Osaki said. "He is drained."

"Has Aerios been sentenced?" Adrestia questioned.

"Yes," Osaki replied. "He has been sentenced to being human."

"Who is the man on the floor?" Kofi questioned. "Does he need CPR? We should probably call an ambulance."

"Aerios," Ciro panted.

"You spared his life," Ares said with a frown. "Why?"

"Carter—" Ciro panted. "You asked me not to kill him..."

Carter looked at Kofi, who looked completely impressed then stood and turned his attention to Osaki.

"What's wrong with Ciro? How can I help?" Carter asked. "And don't tell me there's nothing I can do. There has to be something!"

"Like I said, he is simply drained," Osaki spoke up. "He was fighting and using his powers to contain the storm, as well as catching falling debris to limit casualties, all at the same time. From what I can tell, no other Shiver has ever done that. Add that to the fact Aerios was third born so his powers are almost as strong as Ciro's and it was a hard battle. We must return him to Mount Olympus. Hygeia can help him regain his strength."

"She can come here." Carter nodded. "I want to be here when she does whatever it is she does."

"He cannot be healed on this plain. No human medicine can help him," Ares replied. "It must be on Mount Olympus."

"Why does it...?" Carter stopped himself and pressed a palm to his forehead. He wanted to scream in frustration but the longer he took to make a decision, the worse Ciro could be getting. He glanced down at Ciro. He didn't look well at all. "Fine. But I'm coming with you," Carter said.

"I am sorry, Carter." Adrestia stepped forward and rested a hand on his shoulder. "It does not work that way. You cannot enter Mount Olympus — well, you could but Ciro would never forgive us."

What?" Kofi questioned. "What do you mean?"

"The only way a human can get into Mount Olympus," Osaki spoke up, "is through death. And once you enter, there is no coming back. We have to go alone."

"No. You can't just take him away," Carter snapped. "I need to be there when he wakes up and if he doesn't... He can't be alone. *Please.*"

Adrestia rested a hand on Carter's shoulder. "I know you love him, Carter, and you wish to be by his side in his time of need. But he loves you too, so if you died trying to be by his side, he'd never forgive us. Please understand..."

"Carter, stay here," Kofi pleaded. "They have to take him or he will die. He is coming back — right, Ares?"

Ares did not look too sure and Carter didn't like that. He shook his head and fell to his knees beside Ciro, who was attempting to speak.

"What do you want me to do?" Carter asked him. "I'll do what you ask."

"I have to go," Ciro managed. "But...I shall return. Trust me."

Those words broke Carter's heart, and he hunched over pressing kisses to Ciro's lips.

"I promise," Ciro added. "I promise."

"I will take Aerios to a place where he will do no harm," Ares suggested.

Carter swallowed the lump in his throat and kissed Ciro again and again before backing away and standing. He nodded and watched as the gods formed a circle around the sofa. They looked down at Ciro then toward the ceiling. Though Carter was tempted to push between them and kiss Ciro again, he refrained. White lights shone above each Olympian's head then they shot upward to the sky. Then just like that, they were gone, along with Aerios and Ciro.

"Come on," Kofi said, taking Carter's hand. "I'm bringing you home."

"I don't think I should leave here," Carter replied. "I shouldn't. I mean, I…"

"He's not coming back right now. And I'm sure he won't mind if you leave and come home with me so I can keep an eye on you. Besides, you need to eat something and get some rest."

Carter lifted tired eyes to his brother and gave a small smile. "All right…all right."

Chapter Seventeen

It was more than a week later, and Carter did not know what to do with himself. Work was work, and though he finished some sketches for a couple of firms, helped breaking ground on a few new buildings and had two grand openings, he just couldn't bring himself to sit through meetings. Each day he had to go into the office, he canceled all his meetings and settled for doing things through emails and over the phone.

At home, he searched each room twice, ensuring Ciro wasn't there. Every day his heart would break a little more. A couple of nights he'd gone to Firewall, hoping Ciro would be there but still nothing.

Entering the kitchen, Carter grabbed a bottle of wine and frowned. He returned it to the shelf and reached into the fridge for a beer. Wringing the cap off, he turned it to his head and drank until he tasted nothing but fizz. When the bottle was empty, he walked into the living room, fell into the sofa and pulled a blanket over his body. Sleep would be as it had been since Ciro had been taken—non-existent. Every time he closed his eyes, he had nightmares about what could be happening to Ciro.

"Carter..." Ciro's voice broke through his worried haze.

Carter didn't lift his head. He simply closed his eyes tighter, wanting it to be a sweet dream of peace and forever. A hand brushed his shoulder and he sighed. "Ciro."

Lips skimmed the side of his head then over his cornrows to his forehead. Slowly they moved down his nose to his lips. A warm tongue played about Carter's mouth, licking and sucking at it gently. He opened his eyes and jerked back, only to have his gaze lock with Ciro's.

"Ciro?" Carter reached a hand out slowly. He watched his fingers shake slightly as the tips brushed Ciro's flesh. Heat from Ciro's body burned his fingers causing him to yank his hand back. "Stop haunting me—please."

"I am not a figment of your imagination, Carter," Ciro said. "Can you not feel the heat of my body? Look into my eyes—tell me I am not real."

"You can't be real...they took you away. You promised to come back but..."

"I would never break a promise to you, Carter. Never. Shall I remind you?"

Ciro reached in and unbuttoned Carter's shirt. Carter caught his hand and looked into the eyes of the man he'd come to love. He allowed his gaze to roam Ciro's face, down over his nose, his full lips to his strong chin. Leaning inward, Carter closed his eyes. When their lips met, he sighed, lifting a hand to the back of Ciro's head and sucking the Shiver's tongue into his mouth. He kissed Ciro as if it would be the last time, shoving his tongue deep and reveling in the heat that passed between them. When he felt as if he'd die from pleasure, Carter pulled back and pushed air out his mouth. White smoke left his mouth and he arched an eyebrow.

"You make me hot," Ciro confessed huskily. "You make me burn with passion for you. Please let me touch you — I want to remind you that you are the one for me."

With a small smile, Carter let Ciro ease him back into the sofa and climb astride him, ripping his clothes from his body. He watched, trembling in anticipation, while Ciro tossed the pieces of what used to be his clothes aside. When he was through, Ciro bent forward and pressed his open mouth to Carter's neck.

"Shit," Carter managed, dragging his nails down Ciro's clothed back. "More."

Carter arched, moaning for Ciro, pressing his lover closer to him. His heart leaped each time Ciro's tongue flowed over his skin. He knew for sure he would lose his mind and he didn't care. All he needed was for Ciro to touch him, taste him. Licking his lips, Carter watched Ciro's head move lower and lower until Ciro engulfed him within the hot wetness of his lover's mouth. Gladly, he sunk his fingers into Ciro's hair and pushed his hips upward. He slid into Ciro's throat and groaned with pleasure. "Ciro — Damn! Ciro..."

The sensations magnified when Ciro inserted a finger into him. He scratched at Ciro's shoulder, pulling Ciro up his body until their lips met. "I need you — in me."

"Are you sure, Carter? After everything that's happened..."

"I am so sure..."

Ciro stripped quickly, discarding his clothes to land anywhere. Carter pushed to all fours, bracing his chest against the back of the sofa. He looked at Ciro over his shoulder. The Shiver was busy dressing himself in a lubricated condom.

"Come on," Carter insisted. "Hurry."

Ciro laughed and pressed a kiss to Carter's left butt cheek before aiming for his opening. He inserted the head of his dick, gripped both Carter's shoulders and pulled. The motion impaled Carter, hard and fast. A growl erupted through the room, vibrating off the walls before dying. Closing his eyes, Carter held still for a moment, reveling in the sensation of a real man penetrating him.

Slowly, he moved, pulling Ciro almost all the way off him, only to drive backwards taking Ciro's large member deeply.

The thought of never seeing Carter again had done something to Ciro. It had broken him worse than he'd ever been, worse than having to kill his evil brothers. All he craved for the days he'd been away was to feel the warmth of Carter's heart beat rapidly in love and pleasure against him. As he rode Carter, Ciro knew for certain he was in love—he was desperately and completely in love with the human man on him. Snaking a hand around Carter, Ciro grabbed one of Carter's nipples. He twisted each time he shoved into his man and took great delight in the sounds Carter made.

"I'm almost..." Carter panted.

"Don't hold back," Ciro said, leaning in to kiss the back of Carter's neck. "Let it go and come for me."

Carter trembled then stiffened. A smile crossed Ciro's lips as he dug his hips harder, sinking deeper within Carter's heated core. He pressed his eyes closed and tossed his head back just as Carter clenched around him, squeezing every blissful drop from Ciro. Panting, he slumped down with Carter heavily on top of him. He allowed his powers to lift Carter from the sofa.

"Whoa," Carter called out. "I'm still not used to levitation."

Ciro smiled weakly and made himself a little more comfortable on the sofa before lowering Carter on top of him. When Carter snuggled into Ciro's body, it was the most content Ciro had felt in almost two hundred years.

"Did you miss me, Carter?"

"Yes. I spent almost every waking moment hoping to see you pop into my bedroom or my office. But you never did."

"I am sorry I was away so long. I was healed then had to put Aerios in a place where he would not cause any more trouble."

"He is human—can he remember being a Shiver?"

"He will remember everything but will not have the power to do anything about it. It wouldn't be a punishment if he could not remember. Aphrodite said I might as well have killed him because now he is in his own personal hell. He will now have to live and work as a human being—the very people he detested so greatly. I could think of no better punishment than that."

"I am glad you didn't have to kill him. There've been too many deaths already, right?"

Ciro went silent then, thinking of the moment he's known the battle was over and Aerios had lost. He'd wanted to sink his blade down, taking his brother's head. It would surely have given him great pleasure since Aerios had spent his life making Ciro's miserable.

"Why did he hate you so much anyway?"

"He believed I was given his birthright."

"I don't get it." Carter shifted to look down into Ciro's face.

Ciro caressed Carter's cheek and smiled. "It matters not."

"Yes—it does matter. Why would someone, even a Shiver, go so out of his way to hurt his own brother? I could never want to harm Kofi, ever. There's just this love brothers are supposed to have for each other."

Ciro eased a hand behind his head and took a breath. "I was born first," he explained. "The first from a cursed union. Since I was the first son, I received the brunt of the curse—the strongest powers. On this planet, they would call me the biggest freak, but my brother thought I did it on purpose to punish him."

"How does that even make sense?"

"I know not." Ciro feathered a kiss over Carter's forehead. "But in his twisted mind, it made perfect sense. The thing was, he did not want me dead—he wanted me to suffer. If I had not done something, he would have come after Kofi and it would have killed me if he hurt you."

"Because Kofi meant something to me. He would hurt me so I would turn my back on you, knowing very well how devastated you would be?"

Ciro nodded. "For all the heartache and all the trouble and the pain—I didn't just want to hurt him. I wanted him dead. But I could not take the chance that you would change the way you looked at me."

"And how is that?"

"With heat—with a kind of softness I have been lacking all my life. I cannot let you look at me as less of a man for you."

Carter kissed his nose. "I don't think that could happen. I would understand."

When Carter rested against him again, Ciro sighed and asked, "Could you learn to love me, Carter? Could you see me as the man you would want to spend the rest of your forever with?"

Looking down at him again, Carter said, "But I can't spend the rest of my forever with you."

"Why is that?"

"You are immortal. I am human."

Ciro laughed. "Which means even after you die—I shall be by your side. After your death, the doors to Mount Olympus open and you can walk right in."

"You make it sound so easy. What if I end up spending my eternity with your other brother, down there?" Carter pointed.

"Hades is my brother. All I have to do is ask." The smile Carter gave him made his body light as the air. "So, could you love me?"

"Loving you wasn't hard, Ciro. But we just have to see where things go from here. I cannot make promises like this now."

"As long as you smile like that at me all the time— all is right with my world."

Chapter Eighteen

Carter Olabasu walked into the house and closed the door behind him. "Kofi!" he called, kicking off his shoes and dumping his jacket by the door. He walked through the foyer. "Kofi?"

"In the kitchen."

Carter walked in, dropped Kofi's mail on the counter then made a beeline for the fridge. With the door open, he stuck his head in to find a bottle of juice. For a second he debating grabbing something else but gave up, closed the fridge and climbed to a stool wringing the cap from the bottle. After a long drink, Carter placed his drink on the counter.

"So? How are things with Ciro?" Kofi asked.

"They're fine—he asked me if I could learn to love him."

"I hope you said yes. I mean, the guy's brothers are pains in the ass, to say the least, but he can protect you and he has family and friends who seem to do anything just because he asks them to."

"Of course. The truth is—I think I already love him. It's just that I'd already freaked you out with the gay thing, then the Shiver thing. I feel like I need to give you time to get used to all of it before I spring another to the pile, you know?"

Kofi laughed. "Don't use me as your excuse." He reached for one of the letters. "I am all right with you being gay. The Shiver thing is a tad strange, but I know it's real—just like I know what you're feeling for this Shiver is real. Don't just go with your heart. Use your head on this one too then find the happy medium. I will be happy with it if you're happy. But super being or not, if he hurts you..."

Carter met Kofi's stare and smiled. "I know."

After reading the letter, Kofi made a face and crumpled it into a ball. Carter arched an eyebrow.

"What's in the letter?"

"They're trying to give me another credit card on top of the two I already have. If so many things didn't require a credit card, I wouldn't have any in the first damn place. Who needs that stress?"

Carter laughed.

"Well, little brother," Kofi said, peeling himself off the stool. "What does one feed a Shiver?"

"Regular food. Don't be so worried about it. If you cook it, he shall eat."

Carter helped his brother prepare dinner. They finally came up for air two hours later when the table was set and ready for Ciro. Carter's nerves kicked in then. Kofi must have sensed it, for he poured Carter a glass of wine.

"Thanks." Carter took a sip. "I know you wanted to talk to me and with all the drama happening around I just haven't had a chance to sit down with you."

"It's okay," Kofi replied. "There's been some stuff going through my head lately that I think I'm going crazy. And now, it has nothing to do with your super man."

Carter smiled. "Okay, we have a little time before Ciro gets here. Talk to me."

"You know how Osaki was my guard for a while? Well I find myself thinking about him—dreams really, and I don't know what it means."

"It doesn't have to mean anything," Carter explained. "You were stressed. You were going through something no one should have to go through. I had some nightmares myself about being forced to disappear and you couldn't find me."

Kofi shook his head. "That's not what I meant. They are different. They are…"

The doorbell rang. Carter watch as his brother jerked around at the sound.

"It's just the doorbell, Kof."

"I'm a sodding mess, you know that?"

"No, you're just paranoid."

Kofi chuckled. "I'm paranoid, but you're just nuts."

"Bite me." Carter smirked. "I'm going to get the door."

"Not my job, but the man outside—well, I can say he would love to."

"You fruit!"

When he opened the door, he couldn't help the urge he had to take Ciro into his arms. He was dressed in all black, except for a black and red necklace. When he turned to look at Carter, the wind picked up and blew his hair from his face. Carter gave in to temptation and stepped out and into his lover's arms. Without a word, he tangled his hands around Ciro's neck and took his lips. He didn't pull back until he felt the need to breath.

"You look so damn good," Carter confessed. "But we have to behave."

"Your brother — I know."

"And you used the door." Carter laughed taking Ciro's hand and leading him into the house.

"Yes — I figured after that little pop in thing I did before, and with all the other stuff your brother has had to digest over the last little while, he'd need some time to get accustomed."

Carter kissed him again then led him into the dining room. He watched as the two men hugged before leaving the room to grab a bottle of wine and the wine glasses. When he returned, it was to laughter from his brother.

He shook his head. "What did you two do?"

"What makes you think we did something?" Kofi grinned.

"Because I know you both."

Ciro laughed. "Don't worry, we weren't plotting your demise or anything.

Carter poured them each a glass of wine and they sat around the table for dinner. It was strange to be sitting with Kofi and a lover. Kofi genuinely seemed interested in getting to know Ciro, and that did Carter's heart good.

"What do you call this?" Ciro asked, jabbing his fork into the bowl.

"That's Fufu," Carter explained. "You're supposed to eat it with your hand. Here, let me show you."

Scooping some Fufu into his plate, Carter shared some greens over it, mixed it with his fingers before lifting some to Ciro's mouth. Ciro hesitated only a moment before wrapping his lips around the tips of Carter's fingers. Carter had to fight to bite back a moan and the urge to crawl over the seats and tackle

Ciro as the tongue flowed over his finger. Instead, he wiped his hands in this napkin and looked to see what Ciro thought.

"That is actually really good." Ciro chewed.

"Well, duh. I made it," Kofi said, sticking some food into his mouth.

Carter laughed. "The ego on this one is amazing."

* * * *

With dinner over and the dishes in the dishwasher, it was a bit strange when Carter excused himself to make a phone call to one of his architects, leaving Ciro alone with Kofi. He couldn't understand it, since it was so late. But he accepted a kiss to his forehead and Carter left them. Silently, Ciro sat on the balcony with Kofi as they sipped beers.

"How strange is this for you?" Ciro questioned.

"Can you read minds?" Kofi asked.

"I am not that kind of god," Ciro admitted. "And even if I could—I wouldn't just go digging around in your head. Human beings are different that way. They do not want someone knowing what they are thinking."

"You got that right..."

An awkward silence ensued.

"Ciro, as a brother, I think I have to say this," Kofi said, shifting in his seat. "Carter is the only family I have left. He, as strange as this might sound, is the love of my life. When the world wants me dead, when everything is falling apart, I have Carter. When all my friends decide they're tired of being there and I'm alone—I have Carter. And I know that no matter what, he loves me more than life itself. I'm saying all that to say this—god or not, Shiver or not, you hurt him and I will find some way to make you pay. Do you understand?"

The raw emotion in Kofi's voice spoke volumes, even though deep down Ciro wondered how Kofi, a human, was going to make him pay. Shaking his head, Ciro took a breath. "That is the relationship brothers are supposed to have. But in response to your statement... I do not intend to harm your brother. And anyone who wishes to try will have to deal with me. There is a certain way he looks at me and that just makes everything better. He stares at me and I fight to be the kind of person — or rather Shiver — he can look up to because I fear that tenderness he shows me may vanish. You and I have something in common, Kofi. Carter is the love of both our lives."

Kofi nodded and took a drink from his bottle.

"But honestly, Kofi. I have waited over three hundred years for this man. I am not about to screw it up. Just the thought of not waking up with Carter there beside me scares me more than Zeus."

"Well, that is what makes humans the way we are. We love like no other."

Ciro laughed and held his bottle up in a cheer for Kofi, who touched his bottle against Ciro's. "Cheers to that," Ciro said.

"What are you two going to do about kids?" Kofi wanted to know. "Do you want children?"

"Carter and I have not discussed that yet. But if he wants children, then we will have some."

"It is not that easy — would you tell them about what you are?"

Ciro nodded. "When they were old enough, Carter and I would have to discuss it first and decide. But that is not something we could keep from them forever."

"I think it's bed time." Carter stuck his head out the door. "You two can keep talking. I just want to stretch my back out."

"I will come with you," Ciro said. He stood and smiled down at Kofi. "Thanks for dinner. I will see you in the morning."

"Good night, you two."

Ciro took Carter's hand and allowed himself to be led through the large house, up a winding staircase of wood with a black banister. Finally, they entered a large bedroom and Carter closed the door. Ciro looked around. The bed, immaculately made, sported beautiful dark red sheets and matching pillows and cushions. Suddenly, he felt like a human teenager on his first date. Pressing his hands against his thighs he looked at the windows, causing them to swing open and the curtains to blow inward.

"Thanks for tonight," Carter spoke finally. "Most men wouldn't have gotten along with Kofi."

"He only has your best interest at heart. He loves you, you know?"

Carter smiled. "Yeah. And I love him too. Listen…" Carter walked to Ciro and rested his hands against Ciro's hips. "I want tonight to be the first step toward having a future together. I know—you already know I'm the man for you. I'm human—give me some time to grow into the situation, to grow into you."

Ciro couldn't help himself. "You already grew into me."

"You're so dirty," Carter accused playfully, lifting his lips to Ciro. "But I wouldn't have you any other way. Anyway, in all seriousness—I guess I am agreeing—no—*accepting* your offer for forever."

Ciro smiled, cradled Carter's face and kissed him. "You have no idea how happy you have made me."

"How about I strip for you and you show me?" Carter licked his lips.

He started removing his clothes, and Ciro levitated away from him to lay on the bed with his arms folded behind his head.

"Before we do this, there is something I wish to discuss," Ciro said, wanting to kick himself. He sat up and inhaled. "Children... Do you want children?"

"Of course — don't you?"

Ciro smiled. "Yes, but I am Shiver..."

Carter stopped and cradled Ciro's face. "We will have children, Ciro — you'll see. Even if we have to adopt, we will have our babies. Besides, you have the hook-up with the Goddess of Love."

"That I do." Ciro grinned, feeling happier. "Good. Now, about that little show you were giving me."

"What about it?"

"Oh, please do carry on — slow down a little. Turn around and show me that ass."

Chapter Nineteen

Carter spent the early morning making breakfast for his man and his brother. He even hummed a little. To think he was with someone who adored him and his brother had no hang-ups about it—well, no regular issues—was grand for him. The urge to jump and click his heels flowed through him but he merely laughed and shook his head. He was way too old for those kind of shenanigans, then again, he was alone in the kitchen. Who would know?

Carter glanced over his shoulders to ensure he was in fact alone before he jumped, clicked his heels and grinned broadly to himself. He checked behind him again—alone.

On his second cup of coffee, he flipped some pancakes and carefully checked to ensure the blueberries inside hadn't popped. He was always very carefully about that. No one liked messy blueberry pancakes. After taking those out, he poured more batter into the large pot, and watched them take form. Kofi had taught him how to make them and ever since, it was one of the only breakfast things he would make when he cooked for his brother. Footsteps coming down the stairs caught his attention and for a moment, his heart. Then he remembered, his man was a Shiver—no one was getting into the house without Ciro knowing.

Turning, Carter waited until the owner of those steps appeared in the kitchen. "Morning." He refocused on his cooking.

"Hey." Kofi yawned and instantly made his way for the coffee. "How'd you sleep?"

"Better than I had in weeks," Carter replied. "It's good to not have to worry about Aerios." He removed the last of the pancakes from the pot and added them to the pile he had sitting on the counter. He then dropped some sausages into the frying pot and rolled them around in the oil. "You know, I can honestly say, for the first time in a long while that I'm happy."

"That's good." Kofi sipped from his coffee before dishing himself some of the pancakes and took a seat by the island. "I need to say something before Ciro comes downstairs."

"Um…" Carter looked toward the door, hoping Ciro would use it to give them a heads up rather than just appearing out of thin air. Carter's heart pounded crazily as he remembered how angry Kofi was at Ciro and all the paranormal crap that was happening around them. Just thinking of what his brother had to say made the racing of his heart worsen. Carter inhaled, held it then exhaled. "Okay."

"He's not a bad guy—just has a messed-up family."

Carter chuckled. He sat with Kofi and the two delved into a conversation. It wasn't anything earth-shattering but a conversation to keep them both smiling. It had been a while since they'd spent a lazy morning, just sitting around talking, and it was long overdue.

"Speaking of whom, where is Ciro?" Kofi looked over his shoulder. "Do Shivers sleep in?"

"I have no clue." Carter grinned. "But this one does. It's probably the first time in a long while he hasn't had to worry about his crazy brother bent on world domination. He deserves some sleep."

"I'd say. Can you imagine having to be on the alert because your brother wants you dead? Damn. That's no way to live for man, or Shiver."

Carter couldn't agree more. He nodded. "Maybe he popped out for a bit to check on Hades and the others. Sometimes he stays away to give us time together—he didn't tell me that but I can feel it."

"That's another good trait. He's beginning to make it extremely hard to dislike him."

"Now why would you want to dislike him?"

Kofi shrugged. "I don't know. Maybe it's because I'm supposed to inherently hate anyone my brother is with—they are never good enough."

Carter laughed aloud then covered his mouth just in case his mirth drifted up to the bedroom. "I see. The brotherly thing."

"You dang right, the brotherly thing."

"I love you for it. But I'll be fine. You'll see. Anyway, I'm going to take him some food in a bit. Even a Shiver has to eat."

"Do they have to eat?"

"He's not a god." Carter froze to think about the question. He'd never really asked Ciro—he'd just assumed they had to eat something. "I think they have to. Okay, food to my man."

"You do that." Kofi chuckled. "It's still so strange to know this man has supernatural powers and that Greek mythology isn't really mythology after all."

Carter nodded. "I tell you one thing—every time it rains, I'm going to think maybe one of his stupid brothers is up to no good again."

"Who you tellin'?" Kofi stood. "I have to head down to the office. I was thinking we should have a barbecue on the weekend—maybe invite the others."

"The others?"

"Yeah. The rest of his army," Kofi said nonchalantly. "I have a feeling this Ciro is going to be around for the long haul, so I might as well get to know the clan—right?"

Carter laughed. "I'll talk to him about it."

Kofi walked around the counter and gave Carter a tight hug. Without saying a word, he folded one of Carter's pancakes, bit off a piece and exited the room. Carter blinked at his older brother's retreating back and pouted at his missing food. Still, he smiled, rose from his seat and plated breakfast for Ciro. He climbed the stairs and walked into the room to find Ciro partially dressed and sitting on the side of the bed.

"Morning," Ciro called, but he had an expression on his face Carter had come to know very well.

"What's wrong?" He placed the plate and coffee on the bedside table. "What's with the look?"

"I have to visit the oracle and it is best to do it before the day gets too old."

"The one who was wrong about your mate? Why would you want to do that? It could have just been an honest mistake."

"Remember the attack on you and Osaki?"

"Yes. Where I crashed the car?"

Ciro nodded and reached for the coffee. He took a sip. "My mother questioned the attacker and he confessed he was sent to kill you by Oracle Gnóseis."

"Well that makes no sense. Why would this Oracle Gnóseis want me dead? I mean sure, she didn't see me coming but maybe it was because you were the first Shiver she ever had to read. Mistakes happen, you know?"

"I do not know. That is what I wish to find out."

Carter wasn't sure that was such a good idea. "Baby, maybe you should just let this go. Maybe it's…"

"Carter, I need to know. I need to know so if this comes up again I can protect you—I know you don't want me to…"

Carter kissed Ciro—partially to stop his words and because he just couldn't watch those sexy lips and not taste him. He allowed his tongue to flow over them before Ciro sucked him in. When they pulled back and Carter exhaled, he could see his breath as if he was outside in the cold. He laughed softly.

"Can I come with you?" Carter handed Ciro his coffee and watched Ciro take a few sips.

"Whenever I go walking into danger…"

"I'll be by your side. Sometimes you'll want to cause a tornado because of my stubbornness but…" Carter shrugged. "That's how human relationships are, Ciro. Once you have one you do nothing like this alone."

Ciro smiled and nodded. "Yes, you can accompany me. She is not on Mount Olympus, so you do not have to die to go with me. But we must go now. I would like to come back and spend some quality time with you."

Carter smiled but accepted Ciro's lips in another kiss that made his cock hard and his whole body boil. He held the back of Ciro's lips, sucking the coffee-tasting tongue into his mouth and moaning with the electricity that caused. "We should go," Carter replied around each kiss. "We really…"

Ciro reached down to squeeze his dick.

"Damn… Ciro don't start this if you're not going to finish it."

"You are right," Ciro laughed. "Let me finish getting dressed."

"Okay." Carter flopped to his back on the bed while Ciro moved around the room. "Kofi wants to have a little get together for us and the rest of the gang."

"Rest of the gang?"

"Yeah—Osaki, Adrestia, Ares, Sisqo—the rest of the gang."

Ciro chuckled. "Yes, I'm sure Sisqo will not say no. The others will come if I ask. That's very nice of him."

"Yeah. I think it's his way of getting to know them and not being freaked out the God of War would be sitting on his back deck drinking a beer or something."

"Well, it is a good way to start," Ciro replied. "Now, let's go see what is going on with Oracle Gnóseis."

Carter stood and Ciro stepped in close to him. He knew they were about to disappear but wasn't sure if it would feel the same as when Ares did it. Instead of asking him to touch his hand, Ciro merely covered Carter's lips with his own in a kiss. Carter whimpered, tangling his arms about Ciro's neck and allowing his lover to drink from his lips almost greedily.

When Ciro lifted his head and Carter looked around, it shocked him to see they were standing atop a hill overlooking white houses with blue domed roofs. "Er…are we in…"

"Greece," Ciro replied, taking his hand. "Come on. We must hurry."

"But it's so beautiful," Carter managed. "Just one minute to take in the scenery."

"After, darling—I promise."

They scrambled down a path leading toward what looked to be a dark cave. At first, Carter was nervous but then remembered this was something they had to do in order for Ciro to be happy, to have some form of closure. Besides, Carter was a little curious about why some old woman he'd never met wanted him wiped off the face of the earth.

He tightened his fingers around Ciro's at the mouth of the cave. Once they stepped in, it was as if they walked through a light-flowing waterfall, but Carter was still bone dry. On the other side of what he would forever call the force field, the place was set up like a palm reader's lair. Bottles hung with strings from the ceiling. A few paintings of eyes on the walls and tall vases with strange objects floated in water. No, this place looked more like a scientist's kooky lab than a palm reader's lair.

"You have invaded my sanctuary," a voice that sounded like it belonged to an old grandmother called. "How dare you!"

"How dare I?" Ciro called. "I have questions, Oracle Gnóseis, and I will not leave until I get answers."

"You make demands from me? No one demands anything from me."

The woman peeled herself from the dark. She gave Carter the creeps with long, graying, frizzy hair and big, white eyes. There was no black in them, no pupil at all. She took a step toward him, but before Carter could react, Ciro moved his large frame before him.

"I make demands of you because I know you will answer my questions. If not, I will make you very sorry."

"Ciro—is this a good idea? Threatening an oracle?" Carter questioned softly from behind him. No good could come of any of what was happening. He heard the anger in Ciro's voice and if he were completely honest with himself, Carter would admit he was a bit scared.

Ciro took a step toward Oracle Gnóseis and she gasped and took a hasty step back. That must have told Ciro a part of what he needed to know. "There is something different about me, is there not, Oracle Gnóseis? You feel threatened by me and my relationship with Carter. You feel so threatened, you tried killing him. Tell me why!"

"When you were born, I was asked to give your reading. It was such a strange thing for me. I had never read a Shiver before—you were first. I am not certain why it happened, but it was too early for your destiny to have been written. Zeus cared not—he said you were his firstborn to your mother and he wanted your reading to be done fast. It made no sense to me he was in such a hurry. After the reading, things started coming together—making a little more sense. I found out some things—the most important of which was that Zeus did not tell me your mother was Thýella. That would make all the difference."

"Why does that matter?" Carter stepped to Ciro's side. "A reading is a reading—no matter who the mother is."

"Why does it matter?" Gnóseis asked, casting a savage look at Carter. "Foolish humans—you claim to be so intelligent, yet you do not see the problem within this. Your mother, Ciro, is the Goddess of the Storm Winds. Storm winds are notorious for being unpredictable. They cannot be controlled. The only person who can control them is Thýella. The rest of us have no clue. You have a storm running through your veins, Ciro."

"What?" Carter asked.

"Do you not feel it when he beds you?" Gnóseis questioned while tilting her head to peer at Carter. "Do you not hear the howl of a thousand storms inside your head? Do you not feel the earth move?"

"Start making sense," Ciro demanded.

Gnóseis looked at Ciro once more, leaving Carter feeling vulnerable.

"Your destiny was not written, Ciro," she continued. "The fates cannot write it for they do not know which direction you will come. By the time I realized what had been done, it was too late. I tried correcting it by cursing a few of your brothers to handle the situation, but my spell collided with Hera's. They became evil and began wreaking havoc on Olympus and Earth. I could not have that—Earth cannot be destroyed, for it is instrumental in too many of our people's lives. Then I saw a chance to kill two birds with one stone. If your brothers were fighting you to begin with, why not get rid of Carter so that we could push your destiny in the way it was supposed to have gone?"

"That is why you sent Aceplese after Carter? You were killing two birds with one stone? You must have known I would not have allowed that?"

"Yes." Gnóseis fell into a tall, dark chair with skulls along the back of it. It was as though her feet had given out and she could no longer stand. "The sniveling little moron cannot do anything right. There is so much unpredictability in your life, Ciro. There is no room for unpredictability within the fates. We did not know Carter would be protected."

"Then that does not make you very bright, Gnóseis," Ciro said coldly. "Of course he would be protected.

My brothers want me to suffer, and this is the man I love. He will always, *always,* be protected."

Ciro stood and listened to the answers he was given. The anger cursing through him was unlike anything he'd ever felt before. "Do you understand that because of you, I have had to kill my own brothers?" he questioned. With the fury inside him came his powers. Released within the room, his energy toppled canisters, broke bottles and downed furniture. The sound of a hundred wind chimes hanging from the ceiling filled the air but not for long. Soon all he could hear was the *whoosh* of the strong breeze surging through the enclosure.

"Ciro," Carter called.

Instead of looking back at his lover, Ciro formed a vacuum of sorts around Carter for protection and stepped toward Gnóseis. Though the fury of a windstorm charged though his veins, his heart was heavy. Ciro tried relaxing but couldn't. His shoulders remained rigid. He balled his hands into fists by his sides and his neck elongated. For the first time since he'd known her, Gnóseis, seemed genuinely scared.

"They were my *brothers*. They were *everything* to me. Now they are dead because you screwed up? They are dead because you cannot understand we are all different?"

"Ciro," Carter hollered.

"You tried to break me," Ciro continued.

He stopped walking a few inches from Gnóseis' seat and leaned forward, looking into the blankness of her eyes. "My life is not written by anyone. I have free will. My destiny is my own choosing…"

"Ciro! Ciro, stop," Carter pleaded. "You'll destroy everything. *Please.*"

"I will say this once...and once only. Leave Carter and his family alone. Try harming any of them again and I will burn your world and your fates to the ground. Do I make myself clear?"

Gnóseis said nothing, and that only served to stir Ciro's anger higher. Debris swirled in a vortex of everything that had been broken then engulfed the room. His hair lifted from his head and fluttered with his rage.

"Do you understand?" His voice echoed off the dense walls of the cave dwelling and returned to his ears as thunder. "Answer me."

"I understand," Gnóseis shouted. "Please, just stop! You are destroying everything!"

She fell to the ground before him, clutching at his legs, whimpering and sobbing, pleading with him to make the funnel go away. Though he really wanted to destroy her and everything she held dear, Ciro remembered Carter was with him. With that thought, Ciro took a step back, and the twister he'd created died. For a moment, everything hovered in midair then fell noisily to the ground in Gnóseis' home. The protection field around Carter vanished as well and his lover rushed forward to take his hand.

"It is time to go, Carter," Ciro whispered.

Epilogue

The sun went down over the mountains behind Carter's house as they all sat around, having a barbecue. It was a lot livelier than any others Carter had had, but he wouldn't compare. All he knew was he was happy beyond belief. His man was learning to use the grill, his brother was playing dominos with the God of War. The Goddess of the Storm Wind and Adrestia were busy learning hopscotch and the God of the Underworld had just taken off to deal with some unruly soul. It didn't get any better than that.

For a second, Carter removed himself from the group and stared up at the sky. It was a reddish orange color, almost as if the sky was on fire. He couldn't remember the last time he'd given himself a minute to take in the sky above him. But since he'd begun dating Ciro, Carter found himself having a new appreciation for things around him. Closing his eyes for a moment, he took that moment to pull himself together, wanting to cry with his happiness. When he looked up once more, the sky was no less beautiful.

The sun had dipped lower but it took his breath away, leaving him feeling so thankful and alive.

Ciro snaked his arms around Carter from behind, pulling his body close. His lover's muscles pressed into Carter along with a very hard cock he'd come to adore so much. He moaned, tilted his head sideways and was rewarded with Ciro's lips skimming his flesh. "Baby, I can't wait to get you alone tonight."

"You must be reading my mind." Ciro breathed against his neck. He nipped, licked and sucked at Carter. "Maybe we should sneak away."

"Damn..." Carter's knees wobbled but Ciro held him up. "No. As much as I'd love to agree with you, your mom is here. We're having family time."

"You are right." But Ciro didn't stop. Instead, he moved his mouth to the back of Carter's neck but instead of licking, Ciro only brushed his lips back and forth. "I know this would have been better in a more romantic setting," Ciro whispered. "Then I remember how close I came to losing you and waiting for the perfect time just doesn't seem right."

"What are you saying, Ciro?"

"I love you, Carter. I have loved you since the beginning of time."

"How do you know?" Carter whispered. "Your destiny cannot be written, remember?"

"I remember." Ciro nibbled against Carter's ear from behind. "I know love is something no one can predict, but you were made for me, I just know it. I feel it every time you touch me—every time your body is against mine. I feel lost with you in the most beautiful, complete way there is."

"That is not possible."

"Look at me."

Carter turned and allowed Ciro to trap him against the deck's fencing. "I'm looking."

"Now, now listen very carefully." Ciro's voice was soft but serious. "Have you ever heard it said that when you have to fight for something — work hard for something, it means more to you?"

Carter nodded.

"I had to fight for you, Carter. Every waking moment of my life has been spent battling my way to you. Now I am here and I do not intend to go anywhere or break your heart, for that would cause me pain I could never bear. Do you understand?"

For a little while, Carter stared into Ciro's eyes then pressed his forehead into Ciro's shoulder. "I love you too, Ciro. I think I've always known — since that night at Firewall."

"But you just let me walk away that night," Ciro teased.

Carter looked up into Ciro's eyes, watching the calm, gray shine back at him with a hint of mystery and mischievousness. "I did not. I turned to look at my brother and you just — vanished. I wanted to talk more — dance with you..."

"Do you believe in love at first sight, my darling?" Ciro wanted to know.

"No. I believe in lust at first sight. I think we fall in lust first and it is so good, we swear it is love. It's not a bad thing, just overwhelming. That feeling then becomes more intense and perfect. That's when we fall in love."

"Does not matter. Whether you believe or not, it was for me and you are here in my arms. Even after all the horrible things I have done, I still found you."

"You didn't do anything wrong, Ciro. I wish more men would do what had to be done rather than running away. No matter what happens, remember one thing…"

"What is that, Carter?"

"You never ran away."

He eased in closer, causing Carter to tremble and when he took Carter's lips, the world exploded in a barrage of beautiful fireworks. Their kisses were always amazing but this one, knowing Ciro loved him? This one was even better.

"Aw, come on you two," Adrestia hollered. "Are you going to play a game with us or are you going to stand there kissing all night?"

"I am partial to the kissing all night," Ciro replied after lifting his head.

"Well you two can continue your smooching afterward," Thýella said, taking Carter's hand. "As the mother of a Shiver, there is one thing I must do before my departure."

"You're leaving?" Carter asked. "I thought Ciro said you were staying the night?"

Thýella smiled. "I thought I was too, but I must see to my storms."

Before Carter allowed Thýella to lead him away, he gripped the front of Ciro's shirt and stole another kiss. "I don't need any place romantic to hear of your love for me. What better place than around the people we love most in this world?"

Ciro caressed his face then stepped back, allowing his mother to stand before Carter.

Thýella touched the side of Carter's cheek softly while speaking in Greek. At first, he felt a little strange about it, but when he turned to see Ciro smiling quite proudly, his fear turned to intrigue. When she stepped away, there was a slight burning sensation against Carter's left hip but after he ran his hand over it, the feeling passed. She then kissed both his cheeks and smiled.

"I will grab us some drinks," Ciro said.

There was a shout of happiness from the backyard and they all turned to see Kofi doing what could only be described as a touchdown dance while pointing at the dominoes on the table. Carter didn't remind him if he'd won it was because his competitors had let him since they were Greek gods and demigods. Instead, he watched his brother do a strange pelvic thrust kick thing, and laughed.

Ciro shook his head and disappeared into the house.

"I am truly happy my son has found you," Thýella said and sat on the deck chair again. She sat with such posture, Carter couldn't help but think of royalty.

"That a fact?" Carter asked.

"Yes. He has been fighting for so long and hurting for so long that sometimes I thought he would never find true happiness."

Carter picked up his glass and sat on one of the vacated seats. He lifted his legs up to the deck's fencing and took a breath. "Everyone deserves some happiness. But with Ciro, it's hard not to make him happy because he does this wonderful thing to my life as well."

"Turn it upside down?"

"That too." Carter laughed. He sat up and turned to look at his lover's mother. Her face was beautiful — her slender body very becoming. Her green eyes shone with a sort of twinkle that told of something more behind it. Atop her head sat the most beautiful set of black curls he'd ever seen. With a quick glance over his shoulder, Carter rested his elbows on the table and cleared his throat. "Your son is the most amazing man

I've ever met. There's something about him that takes my breath away."

Thýella smiled quite proudly. "I'm glad. You two have been in love since the beginning of time, Carter. Sure, the fates could not write anything this good—but it was destined from somewhere. Thank you for a lovely—how do you say…barbecue. We should definitely do this again, maybe next time at my place at the North Shores?"

"Can I actually go there? You know? Without the pesky little side-effect of say…dying?"

Thýella laughed softly. "You have a sense of humor I adore, Carter Olabasu. And yes, you can go to the North Shores without dying. It is right here on Earth."

"I would like that." Carter smiled.

"Right now I have a storm to tend to," she told him.

He rose and hugged her tightly for there was no better feeling than knowing someone genuinely loved him. Another cheer went up from where Kofi was busy playing football with Ares, Sisqo, Adrestia and Koi.

"Koi, I have to leave now," Thýella called to her son.

The group broke up and made their way to the deck just as Ciro returned. Carter hugged Thýella again and allowed her to say a private goodbye with her sons. In the meantime, he sat with Kofi, looking at his brother.

"I have to be going too," Kofi said softly. "I have to head into the office first thing tomorrow about another agency we're trying to buy. I'm not sure we will, but if they can convince me it's good business, I don't see why not."

Carter nodded. He kissed the side of Kofi's head. "Thanks for coming. I love you, you know that, right?"

A sober look filled his brother's eyes, and for a moment, he thought Kofi was going to cry. His eyes watered but he blinked it back and Carter nodded.

"I love you too, Carter. Don't doubt that, okay?"

"I won't. I swear."

After Kofi said his goodbyes to everyone, even giving Ciro a hug, Carter walked his brother through the vast house and out to the front where Kofi was parked beside Carter's new car. He stopped and met his brother's eyes.

"Are we okay?" Carter questioned. "I mean, are we truly okay—I am talking basketball on Saturday mornings, club nights, evenings like this, alone with my new family?"

Kofi nodded. "Yes. These people love you. They adore you. That is all I wanted—I wanted people who had your back and would love you as much as I do. Well, sure no one is ever going to love you like I do, but still." Kofi smirked.

Carter laughed softly. "True. Basketball on Saturday?"

Kofi opened his car door and climbed him.

Carter bent over to rest his elbow on the window after his brother wound it down.

"You're going down."

"Prepare to be schooled, big brother," Carter grinned, stepping back when Kofi started the ignition. "Prepare to be schooled."

Soon Kofi was gone and Carter was left standing in the driveway, staring off to where his brother disappeared. He was so happy it was almost as if he would burst. At that moment, he did jump and fist pump, before jogging up the front steps and making his way through the house back to the deck.

It took a while to say goodbye to everyone. Koi was the last to leave and finally, Carter could get his lover where he'd been aching to get him since Ciro's confession of love — in bed.

"Strip for me, baby," Ciro demanded in a husky voice. "I want to see your body."

"All right, Big Daddy — anything you want."

"I am your Big Daddy? I like that. I like it a lot."

Carter smiled. Pride, love and desire all rolled inside him. It was like drinking the best cup of hot chocolate on a cold day and feeling the heat in the pit of his stomach. It was a marvelous sensation He stripped slowly for his Shiver until finally he wore nothing but air. Ciro stepped forward after enjoying the show and ran a hand over Carter's hip — the same one that had stung a little earlier. He was stunned when Ciro slipped to his knees and kissed it gently.

"This means Mother has given you her blessing," Ciro whispered. "That makes me very happy."

"What does?"

"Look here," Ciro said, dragging a finger over the hip. "Do you see it, Carter?"

Carter looked down, shocked to see a tattoo there. It resembled dark gusts of wind. "A tattoo? I don't remember..."

"Yes, you do," Ciro whispered, rising and cradling Carter's face. "Think back."

Carter did and remembered when Thýella was whispering to him. "What was she saying?"

Ciro removed his shirt then slipped from his pants. Naked as the day he was born, he pointed to the same tattoo now over Ciro's heart, expanding across to his shoulder and a little ways up his neck. It hadn't been there before. "This means you are mine and I am yours," he explained. "Aphrodite was right—you are my true mate."

"So in essence, I've been branded."

Ciro laughed softly, backing toward the bed. "Something like that."

"What does yours mean?"

Ciro ran a hand over his markings and smiled. "It means I have been claimed," he explained, a beautifully naughty smile tugging at his lips. "I will enjoy being claimed by you."

He knew he should be upset about getting inked without his knowledge, but for some reason, he just couldn't find the anger. How could he possibly be upset with such a beautiful, caring being?

Carter shrugged, watching his lover sit on the edge of the bed with his legs apart, his glorious cock rigid and ready to be ridden.

"Are you up for something freaky, my Shiver, my love?"

"With you? I thought you'd never ask."

Carter knelt on all fours and crawled slowly to before Ciro. He nibbled against the side of Ciro's foot then up his leg to his knee before showing the other leg the same attention. Then slowly, he dragged his mouth across to what he truly wanted to suck on. A low rumble filled the room and he looked up to see Ciro pinching his own nipples. The view from that position was breathtaking. Ciro's head was tossed back in a kind of ecstasy arch, his long hair flowing over his shoulders. Every glorious muscle in Ciro's body seemed to twitch with the suction of his mouth and Carter wanted to see more. He sucked, licked and dragged his teeth across the head as Ciro used his fingers to flick his own nipples faster and faster.

"Oh, Carter," Ciro sighed.

He knew then as he lashed his tongue against the hardened shaft, feeling it pulse and hearing Ciro whimper his name, life was finally as perfect as it was ever going to be for he loved a Shiver, who loved him in return.

About the Author

Multi-published Remmy Duchene was born in St. Anns, Jamaica and moved to Canada at a young age. When not working or writing, Remmy loves dabbling in photography, travelling and spending time with friends and family.

Remmy Duchene loves to hear from readers. You can find her contact information, website details and author profile page at http://www.totallybound.com.

Totally Bound Publishing

Home of Erotic Romance

www.ingramcontent.com/pod-product-compliance
Lightning Source LLC
Chambersburg PA
CBHW020432180626
46812CB00003B/1199